A STABLE
RELATIONSHIP

A STABLE RELATIONSHIP

•

SANDI HADDAD

AVALON BOOKS
THOMAS BOUREGY AND COMPANY, INC.
401 LAFAYETTE STREET
NEW YORK, NEW YORK 10003

PRINTED IN THE UNITED STATES OF AMERICA
ON ACID-FREE PAPER
BY HADDON CRAFTSMEN, SCRANTON, PENNSYLVANIA

To my husband, Fred,
who systematically removed all my excuses
and gave me not only the encouragement
to pursue my lifelong dream,
but the little extra shove I needed to get started

Chapter One

Oh, no—not in the mud! Cassy tried to keep from panicking when she felt her horse start to lose his footing and stumble in the wet arena. She leaned forward and threw her arms around his neck as she slid her feet out of the stirrups and swung down from the saddle, the way she'd been taught to do an emergency dismount.

She almost made it. But as her boots touched the ground, she too skidded on the slippery surface. She tumbled backward, sprawling on her bottom in an undignified heap.

Cassy tried to get to her feet only to fall again when her already wet boots encountered more mud as she scrambled for better footing.

"Thanks a lot." She scowled at General, who'd recovered his own footing and stopped a few feet away, turning his huge equine eyes on her as though to ask what she was doing on the ground.

Before she could try to get up a third time, Cassy suddenly felt strong hands come from behind to grasp her waist and set her on her feet. She turned her head and looked into the most striking eyes she'd ever seen.

"Are you okay?" the man in the raincoat asked as he released her and took two big steps around the puddle to grab General's reins.

"Y-yes . . . I think so." Cassy wasn't sure if she was more shaken by the fall or the embarrassment of its being observed by her attractive rescuer. She glanced down at her mud-covered body and realized that her pride was hurt much worse than her bruised derriere. "Thanks."

She watched silently as he ran an experienced hand down the horse's forelegs. *I wonder who he is?* She thought. He seemed to have an air of authority, as though he belonged there. He seemed vaguely familiar—as though she'd seen his picture somewhere. The bleachers had been empty when she'd entered the arena. But she'd noticed a sudden movement there just before the fall.

Cassy couldn't see much of his build under the raincoat, but the man was tall—towering at least a foot over her own five-foot-two. His face wasn't handsome in a classic way but had a rugged virility. The deep blue of his eyes was made even bluer by the contrast of his black curly hair, which was long enough in back to reach under the collar of the raincoat.

"Your horse seems to be okay too," he said, turning back to her. "You're both lucky. It's not a good idea to run your horse in footing like this. I hope you learned a lesson."

His patronizing tone irritated Cassy and her chin came up. She glared back at his grim face. "I don't make a habit of it. But this is my only chance to ride this week," she answered defensively. She grabbed

General's reins from his hand. "Maybe you should have considered the danger of sneaking up on people when they're riding." She tried not to notice the look of amusement that came over his face as he lifted a dark eyebrow.

"This rain gear is hardly camouflage. Perhaps *you* should learn to be more alert to your surroundings." He turned abruptly and began walking toward the gate.

Cassy was too humiliated to respond. Not wanting to mount up again in her current condition, she followed behind him leading General. She was too rattled to have him watch her ride now anyway.

He reached the gate first and held it open as she led the horse through. "Looks like you could use a shower," he remarked dryly to her bedraggled form. "Would you like me to put your horse away?"

"No, thanks, I can manage," she replied, holding her head high in an effort to maintain a small shred of dignity. She sloshed past him in her thigh-high English riding boots and headed back to the barn.

Cassy purposely did not look back as she picked her way through the puddles dotting the normally sandy path. She fumbled with the chin strap on her riding helmet, trying to unfasten it with one hand, but gave up in frustration after a few minutes. Another sudden gust of wind made her shiver and pull her waterproof jacket closer around her. The weather had turned unusually cold for a fall day in Florida. She was glad she'd worn a warm sweater underneath the jacket, and jeans instead of her usual breeches, which had to be hand washed. Although she hated to admit it, the man in the raincoat had been right—this wasn't a good day for riding, even though the rain had stopped.

Luckily she and General didn't have far to go to

reach the warmth and protection of the twenty-stall barn where she boarded him. Friendly nickers from the other horses were the only sounds except for the clip-clopping of General's hooves on the cement center aisle as they headed for the security of his stall.

As she untacked and cleaned her horse, Cassy cast a quick glance out the window back at the arena, but saw no sign of the attractive stranger.

"Okay, General," she said aloud, "you get a re-prieve today. I'm going to see if Mrs. D. will let me take a hot bath. I'll give you a rain check until next weekend." She patted the gelding on the neck, gathered up the grooming brushes and riding equipment, and walked back down the center aisle of the barn to the tack room.

As Cassy was putting away her brushes and tack, she heard men's voices coming from the office in the front of the barn. One was the owner of the stable, Mr. Dobranski, and the other sounded like the man in the raincoat.

Again she wondered who the stranger could be. He was probably just the father of one of the younger students, she decided with a shrug. He appeared to be about thirty, which would mean he could have kids. *And a wife,* she reminded herself.

Holding her shoulder bag in her hand to keep from soiling it against her wet body, she strode out the back of the barn.

Quickly covering the hundred feet to the white picket fence surrounding the two-story brick house where Mr. and Mrs. Dobranski lived, she unlatched the gate and went through.

As she turned to refasten it, she noticed an unfamiliar

red sports car parked in front of the barn next to her gray Honda. She continued up the path to the house.

The Irish setter sleeping on the porch barely lifted his head and weakly wagged his tail at her familiar figure. Cassy knocked and waited for Mrs. Dobranski to open the door.

The middle-aged woman's face was warm and welcoming in spite of Cassy's appearance. "Looks like you took a spill," she said matter-of-factly. "Leave your boots and jacket right there. I'll get you some towels and clean things."

By the time Cassy had removed the requested items, Mrs. Dobranski was back with clean towels and a terry robe. She motioned for Cassy to follow her to the bathroom and waited while she removed her jeans, sweater, and wet socks.

"Okay, honey, you have a nice hot bath while I wash these for you," the older woman told her.

"I hate to be such a bother," Cassy apologized. "But I didn't want to get in my car like this."

"Nonsense. You're no bother at all—you're like one of the family. Now you take your time and relax. You've got plenty of time, since your ride was ruined." She shut the door and left before Cassy could argue further.

The old-fashioned bathroom was well equipped. Cassy noted with pleasure a bottle of bubble bath on the counter next to the claw-footed white tub. She finished undressing as the tub filled, then gladly lowered herself into the sea of warm bubbles. As she soaked, she tried to relax and forget all about her disturbing experience.

Tomorrow was Monday, so she'd be back to work at the hospital where she was a registered nurse on a busy pediatric floor. After work she'd have just enough time to come by the stable to clean General's stall and feed and groom him. It would be dark before she could ride.

But she was fulfilling her dream of having her own horse, she reminded herself. Riding wasn't the only pleasure. Just being out in the country atmosphere of the stable—even though it was only a few miles from town—helped relieve some of the stress of her job.

She found all the routine care of the horses—even cleaning stalls—very relaxing. General wasn't an expensive show horse, but he served her needs. He was eight years old, which was old enough to be settled and a safe trail horse, but still young enough to train for whatever she wanted.

She had loved horses all her life, but her family had never encouraged her to ride. Now, at twenty-five, she was taking riding lessons, and she hoped within a few months to enter her first competition—her lifelong dream ever since her aunt had taken her to a show when she was six.

Greenwood Stables put on a small horse show every month, but as yet, Cassy hadn't felt experienced enough to compete. So far her only teacher had been Mr. Dobranski. But she had signed up for a series of clinics to be taught by the well-known riding instructor, David Carlyle. The first one would be the following Saturday—one of the reasons that she had really wanted to get some more riding practice in today. She sighed to herself. *Oh, well, he'll have to take me as I am.*

David chuckled as he closed the gate to the arena and watched the mud-splattered young woman and horse make their way back to the barn. *She's cute—*

feisty too. I hope taking that spill taught her a lesson in safety, he thought.

She seemed to be a good rider, though. She'd apparently been concentrating so much on what she was doing that she hadn't seen him approach and enter the bleachers. That was good in a rider. The fall had been entirely her horse's fault. Of course, it *might* have shied at his raincoat when that gust of wind caught it, he reluctantly admitted to himself.

He took a deep breath and looked around before starting to follow her. This place sure brought back memories. He'd first discovered the joy of horses here. Mr. Dobranski had taught him to ride, and had taken him under his wing. He owed Mr. and Mrs. D. a lot— probably his whole career. His parents couldn't afford lessons, but the older couple let him pay for them by working in the barn.

That was why he'd jumped at the chance to teach a clinic here, even though he could have made more money somewhere else. It was payback time.

The familiar scent of hay mixed with horses and leather greeted him as he entered the barn. The office door was open and he stepped inside.

"David!" The older man rose from behind the desk and came to envelop him in a bear hug. "Welcome back, son."

David laughed as he returned the hug and stood back to observe his host. Mr. Dobranski hadn't changed much in the five years since he'd last seen him. A few extra pounds around his generous middle, maybe, and a few white hairs that had been gray before. But his faded blue eyes were as warm as ever.

"It's good to be back." He took the seat in front of

the desk while Mr. Dobranski returned to his chair behind it.

"You look great," the older man said. "How's your leg?"

"Not bad." He shrugged. "It acts up a little in weather like this, but nothing I can't handle." He raised the leg in question and rested it on his opposite knee. He frowned slightly. It was starting to throb a little, now that he thought about it.

"Need something for pain?" Mr. Dobranski asked astutely.

David shook his head. "No, it's not bad. I quit taking pain pills about six months ago, when I realized the real pain wasn't in my leg."

Mr. Dobranski leaned back in his chair and studied his young friend for a few minutes before speaking again. "You know, I never met Rhonda, but I sure was sorry to hear that you split up."

"Don't be. I'm not." David's lips curled in a rueful smile.

"Are you sure?"

David gave a disgusted snort as his eyes met the other man's sympathetic ones. "Of course I'm sure! She dropped me the minute I got hurt. I woke up in the hospital to find out she didn't pull out of even one competition. Not one! She was out on the show circuit again that same night."

Jim shook his head sadly. "Didn't she know how badly you were hurt?"

"She knew. She was there." David stared at his leg without seeing it, as he massaged his ankle. After a few minutes of silence, he glanced back at Mr. Dobranski. "Anyway, it's over, and I have no desire to go back to show jumping. Teaching is much more rewarding.''

''Well, whatever the reason you gave up competition, we're sure glad you're here.'' Mr. Dobranski smiled and pulled out a clipboard. ''We'll keep you busy too. All of your clinics are full.'' He handed the list to David.

''Great. That's just what I need to keep my mind off things.'' *Like women,* he thought to himself. He glanced at the list of names. ''Who was that riding in the arena when I got here?''

''Was she riding a big dark bay gelding?''

''Yeah.''

''That would be Cassy Collins. She hasn't been riding very long, but I think she'll be good. Especially when you get done with her.'' The older man winked at him.

David raised his eyebrows. ''She signed up for my clinic?''

''Oh, yes, she was one of the first. She's a very good student.''

''Really? She seems kind of cocky.''

Now Mr. Dobranski raised his brows. ''Cassy?''

David shrugged as he continued to study the list. ''Well, we didn't meet under the best circumstances.'' He stood up and extended his hand to the other man. ''Thanks for asking me to come, Mr. D. I'm looking forward to working here.''

Mr. Dobranski took his hand. ''Glad to have you back, even if it is just temporary.''

By now the bathwater was getting cold. Regretfully, Cassy pulled the plug and stepped out of the tub. She toweled dry and put on the large robe Mrs. D. had provided.

As she combed out her shoulder-length mahogany brown hair, she reflected on how lucky she had been to find a stable run by such a nice couple. She had begun taking lessons there shortly after landing the job at Community Hospital and moving from her small Florida hometown to the nearby larger city of Orlando.

She'd seen the sign on the gate while driving by the stable, and on a whim stopped to see if they had any lessons for beginning adults. The couple was so warm and friendly she was immediately drawn to them. Their own children were grown, but they treated all the kids who took lessons there as though they were adopted sons and daughters.

Within a few months, they had convinced Cassy she should have a horse of her own. The young girl who owned General Lee moved away, and on the Dobranskis' recommendation, Cassy bought him. They made her an affordable offer on board so she could still continue taking lessons. She couldn't imagine what her life would be like without her horse and the joy of going to visit him.

Of course, there wasn't much time for a social life. Cassy knew her overly protective parents would have preferred she continue to live with them until she married, as her older sisters had. But none of the men she met in her hometown interested her enough for a lasting romance. She had long ago decided that she would stop looking for Mr. Right and get on with her life.

Now, busy with her job and the stable, she didn't get much opportunity to meet eligible men. Her co-workers sometimes fixed her up with blind dates, but they'd all been disasters. Some of her friends had accused her of being too picky. But she refused to waste her time on someone she didn't care about. She would rather be alone than settle for a relationship without genuine love. So for now, she was content to have her independence and put her love life on hold.

Cassy finished combing her hair and let it fall in soft waves over her shoulders. She gathered up her things and went in search of Mrs. Dobranski, who could usually be found in the kitchen.

She smelled the aroma of freshly brewed coffee as she emerged from the hallway to cross the family room. Sure enough, the older woman was pouring a cup as she came into view.

"Your clothes aren't quite dry yet, Cassy," she said. "But come sit and have a cup of coffee. You can meet David."

"David?" Cassy asked, puzzled. Her heart leapt as she rounded the corner and saw the figure perched on the stool at the counter. Although the raincoat was gone, she quickly recognized the distinctive profile of the blue-eyed man from the arena. He was holding a cup of coffee in one hand and one of Mrs. D.'s blueberry muffins in the other. His navy pullover stretched over a broad chest, and well-fitting jeans over trim hips proved, that he lived a rugged, outdoorsy life. Her pulse raced as she looked once again into his piercing eyes.

"Well," he said dryly, his eyes twinkling as they raked over her small form clad in the huge terry robe, "it looks like you took my advice."

Chapter Two

"Have you two already met?" Mrs. Dobranski asked, looking puzzled as she glanced from one to the other.

"Not officially," he answered, putting down the muffin and coffee and wiping his hand on a napkin. "I believe this is the young lady I fished out of the pond in the arena." The corner of his mouth quirked slightly as he rose and extended his right hand. "Hello. I'm David Carlyle."

Cassy flushed with embarrassment at the reminder of their first encounter. She took his hand and shook it, her tiny hand dwarfed by his strong, firm grasp. "Cassandra Collins. I'm happy to meet you." She forced a smile and withdrew her hand. "I've signed up for your first series of clinics," she added, recognizing his name. "I hope you'll still take me after what you saw of my riding." She was trying hard to regain her composure after the shock of finding out who he was.

His eyes showed a hint of amusement, but his voice

was serious. "If I refused all students who fell off, I'm afraid I wouldn't have many left." He turned back to his seat. "I'm sure it's hard to believe, but my horse and I have been known to part company in the middle of a ride now and then."

Cassy caught a glimpse of pain cross his face before he sat back down on the stool, and she wondered if it was physical or emotional. She remembered hearing he had given up a promising career as a show jumper after a bad accident in which his horse was killed. It had been only after months of physical therapy that he'd been able to ride again.

"Please join us, Cassy," her hostess invited, gesturing toward the extra cup of coffee on the counter. Cassy hesitated, noticing it was in front of the empty seat next to David Carlyle. But she saw Mrs. D. had already added milk the way she liked it and was starting to pour herself a black one.

"Thanks, but just till my clothes are dry." Cassy took the next seat, leaving the one beside David empty. She moved the coffee over so it was in front of her.

"Ooh—my favorite." She took a muffin from the plate Mrs D. extended to her.

The older woman was standing on the other side of the counter. She looked speculatively at Cassy while she took a sip of coffee before speaking. "David was telling me he's thinking of leaving Texas," she said. "I'm trying to talk him into moving back to Florida."

Cassy had just taken a bite of muffin, so she didn't reply as she turned to look at him. He was drinking his coffee and his profile showed an unreadable expression.

She swallowed before nervously asking, "Are you just visiting here while you teach the clinics?"

He put down his cup but didn't look up. "I'm staying at Pine Haven, a friend's ranch, while I do clinics at several stables and riding academies in the Orlando area. So far I'm booked for two months. If I find there's enough interest in my teaching to support me, I may stay permanently." He smiled at Mrs. D. "If everyone makes me feel as at home as you have, I may never want to leave."

His smile changed his whole face. He certainly was a charmer. Cassy saw that Mrs. Dobranski was practically glowing from his praise. *I'd better watch it with this guy,* she thought.

Just then the dryer buzzed.

"Sounds like your clothes are dry," their hostess said, glancing at Cassy.

"I'll get them." Cassy jumped to her feet. As she stood, the robe parted, exposing part of her bare thigh. She quickly pulled it closed and glanced at David to see if he'd noticed. The corners of his mouth turned up slightly with a suggestion of amusement as he raised one eyebrow and lifted his eyes to meet hers.

She turned and stalked out toward the laundry room. After she'd retrieved her clothes, she walked back past the kitchen to the bathroom. But both Mrs. Dobranski and her visitor were deep in conversation and didn't appear to notice her as she went by. She took her time changing, not anxious to face her new teacher again. *That's all he is,* she reminded herself, *my teacher.* But even so it was going to be hard to concentrate on her lessons. She couldn't remember the last time she'd been so attracted to a man.

When she finally returned to the kitchen, Cassy was both relieved and disappointed to find David gone.

Mrs. Dobranski was busy putting away dishes in the

dark oak cabinet over the serving counter. She smiled when she saw Cassy returning. ''Please come finish your muffin, dear,'' she said, motioning toward Cassy's plate still on the counter. ''I'll reheat your coffee.'' She picked up the pot and added to Cassy's half-empty cup.

''Only if you'll join me.'' Cassy slid onto her former seat.

''You talked me into it.'' The older woman grinned as she brought her cup and took the seat on the end vacated by David.

''Did Mr. Carlyle have to leave?'' Cassy asked, trying to sound casual. She picked up the creamer and added some to her coffee.

''Yes, he had to check in at Pine Haven,'' Mrs. Dobranski said. ''Poor man,'' she added, shaking her head. ''I knew him as a kid, and he's had some tough times since leaving Orlando.''

''How do you mean?'' Cassy asked before taking a bite of her muffin. ''Didn't he become a famous show jumper?''

''Well, yes, but I think that caused him more pain than pleasure. Now he just doesn't seem to have the same zest for living. He was always so full of life, ready to try anything. He was such a ladies' man that we were really surprised when he got married.''

Cassy tried not to let disappointment show in her face as she heard this bit of news. ''Was that before the accident?'' she asked.

''Oh, yes, and it fell apart right afterward. Rhonda is a show jumper herself. In fact, that was how they met. During the two years they were married, they traveled the show circuit together. But she wasn't the type to stay home and nurse an invalid husband. She met someone else while David was still in physical therapy. He didn't fight the divorce; he's too proud for that. But I'm sure it made him bitter, probably more so than the accident.''

"He hasn't married again?'' Cassy asked casually. She had finished her snack and coffee, and rose to put the dishes in the sink.

"No. I think he's going to be very careful not to make the same mistake again.'' She smiled conspiratorially and winked at Cassy. "Of course, he may just need the right woman to fall in love with.''

Cassy turned away and pretended not to know who she was talking about. "Well, I hope he doesn't take out his frustrations on his female students,'' she said, picking up her purse. "Thanks for the bath and coffee, but now I really need to get home. I'll feed General on my way out.''

"You're quite welcome, dear. See you tomorrow!'' Mrs. Dobranski called to her.

Cassy slipped out the door with a final wave. She pulled on her wet boots and jacket, which were waiting on the front porch. "Don't bother to get up, Red,'' she said to the dog still resting there. She stepped over him and walked back through the gate and on to the barn to finish taking care of her horse. It wasn't raining, but the sun still hadn't come out and the air was chilly. She was glad it wasn't far to the back entrance of the barn.

Although the double barn doors were open at both ends, inside it was warm and welcoming. Several of the horses on either side whinnied as Cassy passed them going down the center aisle. She stopped to pat and speak briefly to each of the friendly ones who stuck curious noses through the bars on the top half of their stall doors.

By now it was five o'clock—feeding time for all the horses. Several of the other owners were already feeding, cleaning stalls, or grooming their horses. Mr. Dobranski was there too, taking care of the school horses he rented out for lessons and trail rides. Most of the people were friendly but didn't waste time talking to one another. There was too much work to do.

Cassy greeted each as she passed, but went directly to the feed room to measure out General's grain mix. She took it to his stall where she found him already munching on one of the stalks of hay Mr. Dobranski had given each of the horses.

"Here you go," she said, dumping the grain into his feed bucket. General ignored her and immediately buried his nose in his dinner.

Now that it was time to leave, Cassy was reluctant to go out in the cold and face the lonely drive back to an empty apartment. She stopped outside the office to look over the bulletin board.

As usual, it was covered with pictures of people and horses from Greenwood placing in various horse events, news articles about the horse world, ads for horses and equipment for sale, and schedules for upcoming events.

She noticed that all ten places in David Carlyle's clinic were filled for her Saturday-morning class. It was a good thing she'd signed up early. He was a well-known teacher, in demand all over the country. If she was to become an accomplished rider, he was the instructor she needed. Now she'd just have to worry about how to learn from him without getting personally involved!

The rest of the week passed quickly as Cassy went to work each morning at the hospital, went home briefly to change and unwind a little, then to the stable to take care of General. Although she looked for David's little red sports car each evening when she went to Greenwood, she didn't see it or him again.

Saturday morning, she arrived an hour early for her nine-o'clock lesson. It hadn't rained any more all week, so the arena had finally dried out. The sun was shining, though the air was cool and brisk—a perfect fall day.

She was wearing her tan riding breeches with a long-sleeved flannel shirt, jacket, boots, and riding helmet—all typical for an English riding lesson. Her hair was once again tied back in a ponytail and tucked in her hat. The only extra attention she'd given her appearance was to add a touch of modest makeup. Several of the men she'd dated had told her they liked the sprinkling of freckles across her nose, which made her look younger than she was. She was satisfied with the way she looked—she was an attractive woman and her trim figure was enhanced by the tight-fitting breeches.

Inwardly, Cassy was a bundle of nerves—not only because she was having a lesson with a well-known teacher, but because she was also attracted to him. *You're acting like a teenager with a crush,* she scolded herself as she parked her Honda. Her heart skipped a beat at the sight of David's red Miata already there.

Drawing a deep breath, she went into the barn. She saw David as soon as she came in sight of the office door. He was perched on the edge of Mr. Dobranski's desk, his legs stretched out in front of him and crossed at the ankle. Today he was dressed in English riding apparel: tight-fitting tan breeches, knee-high black boots, and a white tailored shirt. Only the helmet was missing, which Cassy noticed was on top of the desk. In one hand he was holding a clipboard to which he referred as he talked. Cassy couldn't see who was with him. He looked up and nodded absently toward Cassy as she passed. *You're just another student to him,* she thought sadly. She didn't stop but went on to the tack room to get General's saddle and bridle.

As Cassy was brushing her horse, her friend Wendy peeked in. She was a cute blonde with short curly hair and a body that was the envy of her friends. Her big blue eyes usually shone with mischief, but she was well liked at the stable for her sunny personality. Her horse, Freckles, was the Appaloosa mare stalled next to General. The two horses got along well, which made it easy for their riders to be friends too. Wendy was a few years younger than Cassy and was studying to be a hairdresser. She was also single and was frequently teased about being a flirt.

"Have you seen our instructor?" she was gushing to Cassy now. "He's gorgeous! I heard he's single too."

"Don't let that fool you—he's going to be tough," Cassy answered as she picked up the saddle pad and placed it on General's back.

The petite blonde was leaning against the stall door, grinning. "Maybe he'll give me some private tutoring."

"Suit yourself." Cassy continued to work. "I plan to try to learn as much as I can to become a better rider." She finished the saddle and picked up the bridle, holding the snaffle bit in her hand for a moment to warm it before asking General to accept the cold metal in his mouth. "Are you ready to go?"

"Yes, Freckles is all tacked up. I'll meet you in the arena." Wendy disappeared again and Cassy finished putting on General's bridle and led him out to the riding ring, where Wendy and several of the other riders were already warming up their horses.

Cassy checked her girth, tightened it, then mounted and began to follow the other horses around the ring.

A few minutes later, she saw David approaching the arena. She continued to ride on and concentrated on her seat, trying to remember all the things she'd already been taught.

When he reached the center of the ring, David lifted the megaphone he was carrying to his mouth and asked the riders to line up in front of him.

All ten students quickly brought their horses over to stand in a line facing their instructor. Cassy noticed she was the oldest in the group, with some riders as young as ten or twelve. Like herself, they had all done some riding before.

Cassy took a place next to Wendy, between Freckles and a white horse on the end of the row.

Their instructor set the megaphone down on the ground and began speaking, his strong, deep voice reaching them all without it. "For those of you I haven't already met," he said, looking down the row, "I'm David Carlyle. I'll be teaching you for the next eight weeks. During that time I'll be doing whatever I can to make you better riders. Some of you may think I'm too hard on you. I'll be tough on everyone. I intend to point out every mistake you make, and most of you will make plenty before we're done."

He paused, looking up and down the row as there was a ripple of nervous laughter. "But we'll be successful if you're willing to listen and work to correct those mistakes. There will be lots of things to remember, and I don't expect instant results. Hopefully, by the time you finish this series, you'll be ready for my intermediate clinic—if you're not tired of me by then and you're willing to continue.'' Another round of chuckles went down the line. He strode to the first horse at the opposite end of the row, and began saying something to its rider. After a few moments, he moved down to the next one.

While he spoke briefly to each in turn, Cassy was able to hear enough to know he was asking about previous riding experience. A couple of times he appeared to be correcting hand position, and once he shortened a student's stirrups. She could see several of the students change their body position as he talked to them. For a few, he placed his hands on their booted legs and physically repositioned their feet.

Cassy watched with amusement as Wendy unabashedly flirted with him and he appeared to ignore it. She waited patiently while he finished giving Wendy instructions on her hand position, then turned and walked toward Cassy's left side.

But General, sensing her nervousness, started to get restless. He tossed his head and tried to prance in place. Cassy frowned and concentrated on calming her horse.

Suddenly David was next to her, placing one large hand on General's neck and the other over Cassy's own two hands where she grasped the reins.

''Hello, Cassy.'' His mouth quirked slightly as he looked into her eyes. ''It's okay,'' he said, noticing her sudden intake of breath. ''I won't bite.''

Cassy glanced at him quickly and saw his eyes were sparkling with humor. She nodded and took a deep breath as she tried to ignore the excitement coursing through her. Her heart raced as her eyes locked with his. She swallowed and sat up a little straighter.

"Since I had a preview of your riding when you didn't know I was watching, I can point out what I've already seen."

"Uh-oh." Cassy groaned with a nervous laugh. "That wasn't exactly one of my better rides."

"Except for the way it ended, it wasn't that bad." He walked to the rear of her horse, studying them both with a critical eye. "You have a good seat and hands, but you need to work on your legs." He walked up to stand even with her knee on her right side. Placing his left hand on her thigh just above the top of her boot and grabbing her ankle with his right, he turned her leg slightly in toward General's side.

Again Cassy forced herself to listen to his words.

"You need to concentrate on keeping your leg right there—no daylight between you and the horse. Keep your toes in and heels down. Don't worry; I'll be giving everyone exercises to help. Although you're already a good rider, I think I can teach you quite a few things."

His voice was firm and professional, but Cassy's heart was still racing. Taking lessons from this man, she admitted to herself, was certainly going to be a challenge—in more ways than one.

Chapter Three

Davidturned to his right and began talking to the girl on the white horse. After a few moments, he turned back to the group. "Okay, walk your horses to the left," he said loudly enough for all to hear. When they were all back on the rail, he picked up the megaphone again and began giving instructions. After they'd gone around several times, he had them change directions. He had already learned all ten riders' names, and corrected them every time he noticed heels riding up, toes too far out, or hands out of place.

Cassy was relieved each time she made it all the way around the ring without getting a criticism—which wasn't often. Several times he called her on her toes pointing out.

When they began to trot, there was even more to remember. Now, in addition to the increased difficulty of keeping her legs in position at the faster and more bouncy gait, she had to post up and down at the proper time—making sure she went up when the horse's outer foreleg was striding forward, and back down in the saddle as the other foreleg began to move.

After several circles around at a trot, David began to order them to do specific exercises to strengthen their legs. He had them ride for a while without stirrups, which Cassy found especially difficult. It was hard enough to keep her legs in position *with* them!

At last the hour was over. He asked them to line up again and spoke briefly to each before dismissing them individually. Cassy was third in line this time so she didn't have long to wait. General stood quietly as David finished talking to the rider ahead of them and then walked up to stand next to horse and rider.

"Well, Cassy, was it as bad as you thought?" he asked dryly, his eyes boring into hers.

"Worse." She groaned. "My legs may never be the same."

He wasn't sympathetic. "If your muscles are sore, you must have learned to do something different. Keep practicing those exercises and soon it'll feel right. See you next time," he said as he walked around the front of her horse and turned to the next one.

Unfortunately, yes, she thought, turning General toward the gate. Outside the arena she dismounted and audibly moaned as she forced her sore legs to walk back to the barn.

"You were right." Wendy came up next to her. "The man is a sadist. I hurt in muscles I didn't know I had."

"Still want your private lesson?" Cassy teased.

"No way—next week is soon enough to see that man again!"

By now they had reached the barn and led their horses to their stalls. As they worked to untack their mounts, they continued to chat about the clinic and the tough exercises their new instructor had made them try. After putting their equipment back in the tack room, they led the horses out to the pasture and turned them loose to graze while they cleaned their stalls. By the time they finished their chores, they saw the advanced clinic riders heading out to the arena.

"Let's go watch," Wendy suggested. "It'll be fun to see him torture someone else."

"Are you sure you're not a bit sadistic yourself?" Cassy asked, laughing. "I guess it would be fun. And we might learn something too."

They put away the manure rakes and walked together out to the bleachers by the arena.

The ten advanced riders had all assembled in the ring and David was giving them opening instructions. He began by meeting each of them much the same as he had in the beginners' clinic. But most of these students were adults. This clinic had only two teenagers, both girls whom Cassy recognized as placing high in the local shows. The others were all at least in their late twenties or thirties, and Cassy knew they were all experienced riders.

This time, David didn't spend much time correcting positions while they were standing, but moved quickly to the walk and trot and then canter, using the megaphone to call out instructions and point out mistakes.

Wendy and Cassy sat quietly most of the time watching with fascination as they saw the other side of their instructor in action. "He's even tougher on these guys," the blonde remarked. "I don't know if I'll ever be ready for this class."

"I don't know if I want to be," Cassy added. "It's much more fun to watch without the pressure."

Her friend nodded agreement. "Besides, this way we can watch him without his critical eye watching us . . . and he's not hard to look at."

Cassy shook her head. "Is that all you're interested in? I thought you wanted to learn more about riding."

"Sure I do—but there's no law against enjoying man-watching at the same time, is there?" Wendy had a mischievous gleam in her eyes, and Cassy gave her an amused smile as they turned back to watch again. She could hardly blame Wendy for being honest. She too was appreciating how virile he looked in his riding outfit.

Now he was having the students ride without reins, picking them up only if necessary. As the horses trotted, the riders stood up in the stirrups using balance to keep themselves centered on the horse. When they'd mastered that, David had them begin arm exercises while sitting in the saddle, but without picking up the reins.

Wendy gave a low whistle. "Do you believe this guy?"

Cassy shook her head. "I'm just glad we're beginners!"

The class appeared to be ending as David asked the riders to line up again and was starting to talk to them individually.

"Well, I guess I'd better get going," Cassy said as they both rose out of their bleacher seats. "I have to work tonight."

"Why? I thought you worked day shift."

"Normally I do. But we can only have one weekend off a month. So, in order to take the clinic on Saturday mornings eight weeks in a row, I had to trade some shifts. I still may miss at least one of the lessons if I can't find someone else to trade with.''

"You'll be here next week, won't you? I'd hate to face Mr. Carlyle by myself.''

Wendy's worried expression made Cassy laugh. "Sure. I wouldn't do that to you.''

By now they had reached the fork in the path, and Cassy turned to take the one back to her car. "I'm coming out for some practice riding tomorrow too. If I can still move.''

Wendy stayed on the path to the barn. "Great. Maybe I'll see you then.'' She waved and continued on her way.

Cassy sighed and walked slowly back to her car as her aching muscles protested in vain.

Exiting the arena, David watched appreciatively as Cassy headed to her car. Even her walk was enticing. She seemed totally unaware of her charm, and that made it even more appealing. Of course, he reminded himself, she was just a kid. He tried to push her out of his mind—he knew he shouldn't be thinking of her as anything more than a student. But it sure made it tough when his female students came in such an attractive package!

She was getting in her car, and he continued to watch while she pulled the elastic band out of her hair and released her ponytail to let her long brown hair fall to her shoulders. She removed her jacket as well, revealing definitely feminine soft curves. He pulled his eyes away. She was much too young for him. It had been hard enough to be professional in class when he was so close to her. If he let himself dwell on her womanly charms, it would be even worse next time.

She had talent as an equestrienne, and he needed to try to help her reach her potential.

The day after her lesson, Cassy could hardly move without her muscles protesting. But she practiced riding during both her days off that week, as well as doing the leg exercises David had suggested be done at home. Each day was a little easier and, by the end of the week, she was looking forward to the challenge of another clinic lesson.

She arrived early to allow herself plenty of time to warm up. All was going well until David strode purposely into the ring. Once again he looked dashing in English riding apparel.

After noting his arrival, Cassy deliberately avoided looking at him. But her pulse was racing, and General, sensing something was amiss, began to prance nervously. The more she tried to slow him down the faster he went.

"I said *walk* your horses." David's voice blared through the megaphone.

Cassy chanced a sheepish glance at the center of the ring. Just as she'd feared, David's eyes were on her. She pulled back on the reins, which only caused General to toss his head in protest.

The commanding voice once again came through the megaphone. "Miss Collins, please come to the center of the ring. The rest of you continue to walk on the rail."

Self-consciously, Cassy turned General in and they pranced up to David, stopping next to him.

"What seems to be the problem?" he asked quietly.

"I don't know . . . he's usually not like this." Cassy

didn't look at David as she concentrated on keeping General at a stand.

David moved a step closer and began rubbing General on his neck just in front of his shoulder in a circular motion. Within seconds, the gelding dropped his head submissively and stood calmly.

Cassy looked at David in amazement. "How did you do that?"

"This is where their mothers nuzzle them," he said as he continued to demonstrate. "Gets them every time," he added, winking at Cassy.

She blushed. When he's being nice he can be so charming. . . .

"Now we need to work on *you*." He took a step back till he was right next to her and placed his hand reassuringly on her thigh. "Your horse can tell when you're nervous. Take some deep breaths and then breathe out slow and even."

Cassy tried to follow his advice, but his touch was definitely not calming her.

He moved his hand from her thigh to grasp her hand, which still held a rein. It felt especially tiny in his large one, and the gesture helped to make her feel safe and secure. She chanced a look into the depths of his eyes and felt herself melting. She could gaze into those eyes forever. . . .

Time seemed to stand still as neither spoke for a moment.

Finally David continued. "The first time I saw you ride you didn't know anyone was watching and you were concentrating solely on your riding. I want you to do that now, okay?"

Cassy nodded and looked away.

''Good. Let's try it again,'' he said, giving her hand a final squeeze before he stepped aside.

Cassy straightened her position in the saddle and took slow, even breaths before cuing General to walk.

''Perfect,'' David called to her as she rejoined the riders on the rail.

The rest of the lesson went smoothly. David could see improvement in all the riders when they reviewed movements from the first lesson. He got the expected protests from them about the new exercises he made them try. Once again they were all tired and sore by the end of the hour.

The next two clinic sessions were much the same. Each time, they were put through a series of rigorous exercises to strengthen their muscles and increase balance. David continued to point out every mistake as soon as he caught it. But each time it got easier, and the muscle soreness eventually went away. Cassy found herself enjoying the lessons in spite of the stress of trying for perfection. Each time David touched her to correct her hand or leg position, she reminded herself it was strictly professional. She did her best to ignore her unsettling reaction.

By the end of the fourth lesson, she was feeling much more confident. When she had a day off during the week, she spent most of it at the stable practicing with General. If Wendy was there too, they would sometimes take a trail ride together through the woods and fields surrounding Greenwood. The blonde had a new boyfriend, so she was full of news about her romance. Her only comments about Mr. Carlyle were now about his tough lessons.

*   *   *

The Monday after her fourth clinic lesson, Cassy noticed the red sports car already there when she pulled up to the barn in her Honda. Today she had come straight from work, since she didn't want to waste the time to go home and change. She planned to change into her riding clothes in the office bathroom, so she gathered up her jeans, T-shirt, and boots which were scattered over the backseat of her car.

It was a perfect day for riding. She liked the smell of the stable—cool, brisk air mixed with a horsey scent that wasn't at all unpleasant.

The office door was open, as usual, so Cassy went in.

To her surprise, she found David sitting in the armchair across from the empty desk. He looked up from his clipboard as she came into view.

Her breath caught in her throat when his eyes locked with hers. "Oh, hi . . . I didn't know anyone was here," Cassy stammered.

David laid the clipboard on the desk, appearing slightly startled. His eyes slowly traveled from her head, with her hair neatly pulled in a bun, down past her white uniform dress to her white hose and comfortable white shoes. She'd already removed her cap and left it in her car.

"Where do you work?" he asked, his piercing gaze returning to her face.

"Community Hospital. I was just planning to change in the bathroom, so I could ride before feeding time." For some reason Cassy felt defensive.

"Really? What do you do? I thought you were still in school." He raised his arms over his head and stretched lazily leaning back in the chair.

"I'm an RN on pediatrics. How old do you think I

am?'' She stopped and leaned back against the wall, feeling slightly smug that he obviously had thought she was much younger.

"I had you and Wendy pegged as a couple of teenagers, like the rest of your class. But if you're not only out of high school but nursing school too, I was apparently wrong . . . I'd guess twenty-two or -three.''

"I'm twenty-five. Wendy is twenty-one.''

He raised both dark eyebrows. "Well, I guess I underestimated you both. Maybe I'll have to be a little harder on you in class.'' He smiled and wickedly wiggled his eyebrows.

"Oh, no—you're plenty tough as it is!'' She gasped. At his surprised arch of one eyebrow, she added, "But you're an excellent teacher. We're learning a lot.''

"I'm glad,'' he replied seriously. "You have a great deal of potential as an equestrienne. Mr. Dobranski told me you haven't been riding for long. If you stick with it, you can go far.''

"Thank you.'' Cassy was blushing with pleasure. "I'm afraid I'll have to miss your next lesson, though. I have to work day shift next weekend.''

He looked at her thoughtfully for a moment before speaking. "Are you sure you're not trying to chicken out?'' The left corner of his mouth turned up slightly with a suggestion of humor as he picked up the clipboard and flipped to another page. Before she could answer, he spoke again. "Will you be off by this time on Thursday?''

"Yes, I finish work at three-thirty, so I can be here by four o'clock. Why?''

"I have a five o'clock clinic for beginning adults at Pine Haven that day. You'd have to ride one of their school horses, but it would be good experience for you. They're all at the same level as your regular class.''

Cassy hesitated. ''Are you sure it would be okay?''

''Absolutely. The owner is a good friend of mine.'' He looked back at his schedule. ''In fact, I'll be going there after I finish my kids' class here on Thursday, so you can ride over with me.''

''Okay, thanks.'' Her heart skipped a beat at the thought of the extra time with him—alone. ''Well, I'd better get changed now. I'll need all the practice time I can get!'' She started toward the bathroom.

''Work on those no stirrup exercises,'' he suggested.

''Yes, sir,'' she quipped, giving a mock salute as she stepped into the office bathroom and shut the door.

When she emerged a few minutes later after changing, he and his clipboard were gone. She saddled up General and practiced for almost an hour, then finished her barn chores and went home without seeing him again until Thursday.

On the day of her lesson at Pine Haven, Cassy hurried to Greenwood Stables right after work, bringing her change of clothes with her. When she arrived, she saw a children's class in progress in the arena. David was in the center teaching and, if he noticed her arrival, he gave no sign of it. She quickly changed from her uniform, took care of General, then joined the three observers in the bleachers. She had seen all of them before at the stable. Two were in the advanced class themselves, and they all had children who were regulars at the stable.

''Is Megan in this class?'' she asked the brunette she knew to be Megan's mom.

''Yes,'' Mrs. Davis answered without taking her eyes off the arena. ''I wasn't too sure about letting her do it after I had my first class with Mr. Carlyle. But he's wonderful with them.''

Cassy could tell that the kids were enjoying themselves. And yet they were all behaving perfectly, appearing to hang on his every word. A few minutes later, the class ended. The parents followed their children to the barn to help them untack. Cassy lingered in the bleachers until David dismissed the last student.

''All set?'' he asked when he reached the gate.

Cassy fell into step with him. ''I hope so. It's been a while since I've ridden any horse but General.''

''Well, it'll help you prepare for next week when I'm planning to have everyone switch horses anyway.'' He looked sideways at her. Cassy wasn't reassured by that added information and didn't comment.

They reached the red sports car, and he opened the passenger door for her. He tossed his hard hat and clipboard in the back, then stepped aside so she could climb in. ''Be right back,'' he said. ''I want to tell Mr. D. you'll be with me.''

Cassy settled in the bucket seat, and he shut the door. She had a moment to admire the black leather upholstery as he disappeared into the barn. She took a deep, calming breath. What would it be like riding all the way to Pine Haven together in his small car?

Soon he came back and climbed in beside her. She tried not to be too obvious watching him as he started the car and backed it out of the driveway. He was wearing his usual teaching apparel—riding breeches and boots topped off with a tailored, white long-sleeved shirt. It had been warmer than usual that afternoon, and he'd opened several of the top buttons on his shirt, revealing a tuft of curly black hair.

He seemed to be concentrating on his driving, so

they rode in silence until they reached the main highway.

Finally, Cassy decided to break the ice. "How did your class go? I bet those kids are a handful." She tucked her left leg up behind the right and half turned to look at him.

David gave a deep chuckle. "Oh, yes. I really enjoy it, though. They have a very short attention span, so it keeps me alert. I have to keep the children's classes much smaller 'cause they need a lot of individual attention." As he stopped for a light, he glanced at Cassy. "You work with kids too, don't you?"

She was pleasantly surprised he'd remembered that. "Yes, but unfortunately, they're sick or injured when I take care of them—not at their best."

"You must really have a lot of patience . . . no pun intended," he added as he realized the double meaning. "Taking care of someone who's not feeling well is a difficult job. A lot of people can't handle it."

Like your ex-wife, Cassy thought, remembering what Mrs. Dobranski had told her. Instead she said, "Yes, it's especially hard when they're too young to talk because they can't tell you what's wrong. But luckily, kids usually don't stay sick long. They recover very quickly as a rule, and we try to send them home as soon as possible. It's hard on the whole family when one member is in the hospital. They usually recuperate more quickly once they get home. Of course, if they've been abused—or we suspect they may be—it's really hard to send them home to face the same situation. We're always certain to alert the authorities in cases like that. Sometimes, I really get attached to the kids." She stopped and glanced quickly out the window. He was touching on a sensitive subject.

"How do you handle it when you lose one?" he asked perceptively.

"Not very well, I'm afraid. That's the real reason not to get too personally involved. It's too hard when one dies."

She glanced at David and saw he was nodding, as if he understood, though his eyes were on the road. Finding it easy to talk to him, she continued, "Sometimes the stress really gets to me. That's why I enjoy going out to the stable after work to unwind."

"I know what you mean," David said. "There's something about being around horses that's relaxing. Most of the time," he added with a chuckle. "Horses can be stressful too. I heard somebody say once that he never really learned to cuss till he got on a horse."

Cassy laughed too, enjoying the lighter side of David. She'd never heard his deep husky laugh before. Getting to know him as an equal was exciting.

"Do you like your job the rest of the time?" he asked, returning to the original subject.

"Oh, yes," she assured him. "Most of the kids get well, and it's very satisfying. Probably like when you send a student on to the next level." She deliberately tried to switch the topic of conversation back to him.

"Yes, I suppose so." He nodded but kept his eyes on his road. "Have you ever been to Pine Haven?" he asked after a few minutes.

"No. Is it much like Greenwood?"

"It's not as big. They have boarders and trail horses but I'm the first riding instructor. My friends, Chad and Maggie, bought the land when they were first married and lived in a trailer on it so they could have horses. Eventually, they built a house and expanded the pasture, making improvements as they could afford it. When they heard I was coming to Orlando, they insisted I stay with them, and they finished building the riding ring, so I'd have somewhere to teach.''

"It sounds great. I'm looking forward to meeting them.''

David's voice was grim as he said, ''Six weeks ago Chad was killed in a car accident.''

Cassy gasped. ''Oh, no! I'm sorry. . . . '' She looked quickly back at David, but he was looking straight ahead at the road, his expression unreadable.

"How is Maggie? It must have been an awful shock.''

"Yes . . . it was. She's a strong lady, though, and is doing okay. She's planning to continue running Pine Haven by herself now and is already making improvements. Chad would be proud of her.''

They were turning onto a side road, and David shifted into a lower gear as the abundance of sharp turns necessitated a reduced speed. ''There it is.'' He nodded ahead as they rounded a turn.

Above the entrance to the driveway was a large handpainted sign stretched across two large pine trees on either side of the drive. It read *Pine Haven*. They turned in and Cassy looked out her window to admire the view. Besides the abundant pine trees, there were many native palmettos, scrub and live oaks, and other trees and bushes all left in their natural state.

"It's beautiful.'' She sighed. ''How big is it?''

"About twenty acres. Five contain the house and barns with pasture. The rest is left natural for trail riding.'' He nodded toward a trailer nestled in a small clearing. ''That's where they lived when they first came here. I'm staying there now since it wouldn't be right to stay in the house without Chad.''

Till then Cassy had assumed Chad and Maggie were an older couple, like the Dobranskis. Now she realized that he'd never said how old they were. She didn't have long to wonder.

As they were approaching the house, she saw a woman standing on the porch, which appeared to run all the way around the log cabin. She was facing the back but turned as they approached and came down the steps toward the car.

"Is that Maggie?" Cassy asked, almost hoping it wasn't. She didn't expect her to be so young and attractive. She didn't look much older than Cassy, and her tight, though worn, jeans looked too good on her slim figure. Her black, curly hair was short and framed a friendly, pretty face.

He nodded affirmatively as he reached behind Cassy's seat to retrieve his hat and clipboard. They both opened their car doors just as Maggie reached them.

"Hello, Maggie," he said warmly as he took her hands and gave her a gentle kiss on the cheek. "How are you today?"

"I'm okay. Every day is a little easier." She turned to Cassy and extended her hand. "Hi. I'm Maggie Newman."

"Cassy Collins. I'm so sorry about your husband—David just told me." She took the other woman's hand, wondering at the twinge of jealousy that ran through her as she looked into Maggie's beautiful eyes.

Chapter Four

For a moment, it looked as if Maggie might cry, a hint of tears beginning to well up in her wide blue eyes. But they were quickly blinked away as she smiled. "Thank you. I don't know what I would have done without David."

She turned back to him and said, "I saddled up Lady for Cassy, and she's ready to go. I hope you don't mind that I can't stay, but I have to get to the feed store. I know you have plans for later anyway."

Maggie kissed David on the cheek and walked toward the red pickup truck parked next to them. "Nice meeting you, Cassy. Have a good lesson." She climbed in the driver's seat of the truck and, with a nod and wave at the two of them, she was gone.

"You should be flattered—Lady is her personal mount. Come on, I'll introduce you to her." David started to walk around the side of the house.

Cassy followed. As they reached the corner of the building, she could see the barn. It wasn't as large as the one at Greenwood, but appeared to be much newer.

Several horses and riders were already warming up in a three-rail round pen, which was about half the size of the arena at Greenwood. Most were riding Western, but Cassy noted one other English saddle. She was relieved to see that Maggie had known she preferred to ride English too, when she spotted a buckskin already tacked up and tied to the cross tie in front of the barn.

"This is Lady," David said, stopping next to the horse. "She's a little more spirited than General, but I think you'll like her."

Cassy moved close to the mare while talking softly and allowed the horse to sniff her hand before patting her velvety nose.

After a few minutes, David unhooked the cross tie and led the horse over to the riding ring. "Go ahead," he said, "I'll give you a leg up."

Obediently, Cassy faced the horse next to the saddle and bent her left leg. David cupped his strong hands under her calf and knee. He counted to three as she gave a small jump, and he easily lifted her up.

She settled lightly in the saddle before saying, "Thanks . . . this feels strange," referring to the new horse as well as the completely different tack and surroundings.

"Just takes a little getting used to. You'll be fine," he said reassuringly. He opened the gate and motioned her through. "Go ahead and warm up." He strode to the center of the ring and began watching the other riders.

Cassy started walking around the small arena on Lady. She found her very willing and obedient to the slightest command. After only two circles she felt comfortable enough to trot.

Since the ring was so much smaller, and there were only six students including herself, David didn't need a megaphone. He began the lesson by introducing her to the group and telling them why she was there. From then on it went much the same as her previous lessons with him.

Knowing David a little better as a person now helped Cassy relax. She was starting to realize he wasn't as straitlaced as she'd originally thought. And it seemed to her that he treated her with slightly more respect than when he'd thought she was a teenager.

The lesson passed quickly. Cassy enjoyed riding the little mare. When it was over, she waited until last to leave the ring so David could take her to the barn.

He showed her where Lady's stall was and helped her untack. They talked companionably about horses as they rapidly finished the work.

On the way back to Greenwood, Cassy suddenly realized David had told her he was staying in the trailer at Pine Haven. "I'm sorry," she said. "Are you making this trip back just because of me? I could have driven myself."

"No, actually I had to go back anyway. The Dobranskis wanted to meet with me about business, so they invited me for dinner. Before I left, I told Mr. D. I was bringing you with me. I have a feeling the invitation will be expanded to include you."

Sure enough, when they pulled into Greenwood a short while later, there was a note on Cassy's car asking her to come up to the house.

"Didn't I tell you?" David said with a wink.

After checking on General, they washed up in the barn office bath and walked up to the house together.

Mrs. Dobranski greeted them both at the door and ignored Cassy's weak protest that she wasn't dressed for dinner. "You should know by now that people around here are only out of place if they *don't* have a horsey scent." She laughed.

The table was already set for four. Mr. Dobranski and David sat down and began to talk business while Cassy helped Mrs. Dobranski bring out the salad, garlic bread, and pan of homemade lasagna.

During the meal, David and their hosts told Cassy several entertaining stories about his early riding experiences.

She was surprised to learn that he had taken lessons from Mr. D. as a boy and boarded his first horse there.

The meal passed much too quickly. Cassy insisted on helping clean up while the men talked over second cups of coffee. She overheard enough of their conversation as she cleared the table to tell that Mr. Dobranski was asking David to consider another series of clinics.

She told her hostess about her lesson at Pine Haven while they washed and dried the dishes. "Thanks so much," Cassy said when they were finished. She hung up the dish towel on a hook by the sink. "The dinner was delicious, but I'd better be going."

Mrs. Dobranski stepped to the kitchen doorway and called into the dining room. "David, dear, Cassy is leaving. Would you please walk her out to her car? It's awfully dark out there." She turned back to Cassy. "Call us when you get home, dear. I'll worry about you driving by yourself."

"I promise." Cassy was amused by the motherly treatment. She kissed the older woman on the cheek and called out a quick good-bye to her husband. David rose from his chair and came to meet her in the doorway.

"That was a lot of fun," Cassy said to him as they walked together out into the darkness. "Thanks so much for everything. I really enjoyed my lesson."

"I liked it too. Any time you have trouble making the regular class, just let me know." They reached her car, and he opened the driver's door for her. "Don't forget to call, or Mrs. Dobranski will send out the cavalry." He winked as she climbed in.

"I will. Thanks again." She met his eyes and smiled. His eyes were unreadable in the darkness. She quickly looked away and fastened her seat belt. He shut the door, and she started the car.

Cassy took a deep breath to calm her racing heart as she pulled away. *Easy, girl, he's your teacher. Don't read anything more into it,* she told herself.

David frowned as he turned back to the house. Why had he just felt such an urge to kiss that girl? True, having dinner together had made the evening seem more like a date than the end of a lesson. But she was still his student! He'd had attractive women students before and been able to remain aloof. What was it about Cassy that made him want to grab her and kiss her senseless? He'd had plenty of occasions to see other female students away from class, even others as pretty as she was. But he hadn't felt this way about any of them. He hadn't even liked most of his dates this much. Maybe that was it. He really *liked* her. She was more than just cute. She was a nice person too.

After a quick knock, he reentered the house and found both Dobranskis seated in the living room. He caught an amused smile pass between them as he reached the doorway. Mrs. D. was sitting at one end of the well-worn couch, busily knitting a sweater, while her husband sat in the equally worn overstuffed armchair across from her.

Mr. D. took a long puff on the pipe in his hand and watched the smoke unfurl as he blew it out. "Nice young lady," he said to David before putting the pipe back in his mouth.

David entered the room and slowly lowered himself onto the couch before responding.

Their Irish setter got up from his position at Mr. Dobranski's feet and came over to lay his head on David's lap.

"Well, hello, Red. Do you remember me?" David scratched the old dog behind his ear while he answered the other man. "Yes. She's a good rider too. I think I can have her showing within a month." He sat back on the comfortable couch and pretended he didn't know what they were up to.

"Would you like some more coffee, David?" Mrs. Dobranski asked, setting aside her knitting.

"No, thanks, I shouldn't stay long. But I wanted to thank you again for the great dinner." He turned to look at her and watched her kind, wrinkled face flush with pleasure.

"Oh, you're very welcome. I'm so glad Cassy could join us too. We're very fond of her, you know."

"You're not trying to matchmake, are you?" David tried to look stern but couldn't help being amused at the look of mock innocence she was wearing.

"Oh, no! We know how you feel about dating students. But if you ever change your rule, you couldn't find anyone sweeter." She patted his leg affectionately.

"I'll keep that in mind." He turned to look back at her husband, who was still puffing on his pipe. "I suppose you're in on this too?"

The older man met his eyes levelly. "It was your idea to take her to Pine Haven." He took another puff on the pipe, then slowly took it out of his mouth and held it as he spoke again. "She's special. If you're not interested, make sure she knows it."

David nodded thoughtfully, feeling like a schoolboy

getting a father's warning before taking out the daughter. He knew Mr. D. was right. Spending time with her away from class would encourage her to think they could have a personal relationship. He'd have to try to avoid that.

Cassy discovered that by going directly to the stable after work and changing there she had a better chance of running into David. She began a new routine and found it gave her more riding time, as well as the advantage of sometimes getting to see him teach his afternoon classes.

Occasionally they spoke briefly when they passed in the barn. He was always courteous—but strictly professional. After a few days, Cassy admitted to herself he didn't seem to be seeking her out as she was him. After that, she stopped making any attempt to watch his classes. She spent the extra time riding General in the nearby pasture.

A week after her lesson at Pine Haven, Cassy arrived at the stable after work to begin her usual routine. But as she opened her car door, she heard a child's scream coming from somewhere behind the barn. She jumped out and shoved at her car door, not bothering to check that it was closed.

As she started to run toward the sound, Wendy came running around the corner of the barn and spotted her.

"Oh, good, Cassy, you're here. Come quick!" Wendy grabbed her arm and pulled her in the direction from which the blonde had just come.

As soon as they rounded the corner of the barn, Cassy could see where the accident had happened. She didn't have to ask who was hurt.

Nine-year-old Megan was sitting on the grass next to the tractor used for mowing the pasture, crying hysterically, blood pouring from a jagged cut on her wrist.

Mrs. Dobranski was trying to stop the bleeding with her apron, but the girl was screaming and trying to writhe out of her arms.

Cassy immediately took charge. She reached in the pocket of her uniform for the pair of gloves she always carried, slipping them on while she assessed the situation.

Sinking to the ground next to the girl, she pulled her onto her lap, wrapping both her own arms around her to restrain the flailing limbs.

Mrs. Dobranski gladly relinquished the wailing girl and Cassy firmly clasped a hand over the bleeding wrist. "It's okay," she crooned softly to the child. "I need a clean cloth and some ice."

Mrs. Dobranski got to her feet. "We have some in the office." She started to hurry back toward the barn.

"I'll go with you." Wendy followed the older woman. "What can I do?"

Cassy looked up at the sound of David's deep voice and met his eyes. She'd been concentrating on her patient and hadn't noticed his arrival on the scene. But she didn't hesitate to use her self-appointed authority.

"I need a temporary bandage. My hand just isn't working. . . ."

Immediately David began unbuttoning his white dress shirt.

Before Cassy realized his intent, he removed it and wordlessly tore off a large strip. Hunkering down next to her, he placed it over the wound while Cassy carefully removed her hand.

Cassy quickly but securely tied the cloth around the cut, effectively stopping most of the bleeding. "Let's move her to the office." Cassy spoke firmly, knowing she was the accepted person in charge.

David scooped up the child in his arms and purposely

strode toward the barn. His long strides kept him a few steps ahead of Cassy, and she had to jog to keep up. Megan quieted somewhat, perhaps feeling safer wrapped in his strong arms.

Cassy almost wished she could trade places with the girl. Following behind as quickly as she could, Cassy couldn't help but notice the rippling muscles of David's bare torso.

Embarrassed at the direction her thoughts were taking, she hurried to catch up with him at the barn door. They entered the office together.

David set the child down gently in the armchair and turned expectantly to Cassy, quietly accepting her authority.

Mrs. Dobranski produced an ice pack from the office refrigerator and handed it to Cassy.

She crouched next to the chair and held it on the wound as she continued to console the frightened child. "We need to try to find Megan's mother," Cassy said without taking her eyes off her patient.

All the noise had attracted everyone from the barn. They were beginning to get in the way, crowding around the doorway.

David's eyes swept over them in search of Megan's mother, but she didn't appear to be among them. "We've got everything under control here," he said sternly. "But we need her mother."

The crowd took the hint and began to go back to whatever they were doing before the crisis began. David turned back to Cassy.

She was still talking calmly to Megan, reassuring her that she'd be okay. The hysterical screaming had stopped, and now the child was trying bravely to stop sobbing.

Cassy looked up and caught David's eyes for an

instant and smiled before turning back to the child. Finally, having sufficiently calmed her, Cassy untied the makeshift bandage and peeked underneath it. "It's not deep," she said. "But it's in a bad spot, near her wrist. I think it will need stitches."

That piece of news brought on a fresh wave of hysterical crying from Megan. But Cassy continued to hold her and talk softly to her until once again the girl had calmed to quiet sobs.

Meanwhile, Mrs. Dobranski produced a first-aid kit. Cassy took it from her and removed the necessary antiseptic, gauze, and tape. She calmly cleaned and wrapped the wound, while David watched admiringly.

This was another side of her, showing she was a competent nurse as well as a beautiful one, he thought.

At Cassy's suggestion, Mrs. Dobranski called Megan's doctor. By the time she'd finished the call, Wendy had found Megan's mother.

Mrs. Davis rushed into the office just as Cassy was putting the last wrap in the bandage. "Is she okay?" she gasped, her frightened eyes focused on Megan's face as she ran over to her daughter.

Mrs. Dobranski explained that she'd already called their doctor and he'd said to come right in for the stitches and a tetanus booster. Her husband could drive them.

After thanking them all profusely, Megan and her mom were on their way. Cassy and David stood in the barn entrance and waved as they watched Mr. Dobranski's car drive away.

Mrs. Dobranski's voice came from behind them. "Thanks, Cassy. I'm sure glad you got here when you did."

Cassy turned to smile at the older woman. "Glad I

could help. Megan is a sweet kid. I think she was more frightened by the blood than anything."

"She's not the only one. I nearly fainted myself."

"How did it happen?"

"Apparently she was playing on the tractor and fell against the blade. I'm just thankful it wasn't worse."

"Kids aren't allowed near the tractor, are they?" David asked.

"No," Mrs. Dobranski admitted. "And you can be sure that rule will be enforced from now on!" She reentered the office and David followed.

Cassy hesitated a moment at the doorway. Now that the crisis was over, she could allow herself to think of other things.

David was already picking up his clipboard, which was on the desk. He turned back toward the doorway without looking up. He still wore no shirt, and Cassy couldn't help but admiring his physique.

Suddenly he glanced up and caught her eyes. Cassy could feel herself flushing. *Darn. Why do I let him affect me like that?* she thought. She was a nurse, after all. She'd seen plenty of men without shirts.

"Well, I guess I'd better go," she said aloud, without moving.

A mischievous twinkle appeared in David's eyes, though he remained unsmiling. "I'll see you in class on Saturday . . . and I promise I'll be wearing a shirt."

Cassy could feel herself blushing even more. She turned abruptly and almost bumped into the doorway in her haste to get out.

"See you later, dear," Mrs. Dobranski called to her from behind the desk. The older lady turned disapproving eyes toward David. "That wasn't nice."

Chapter Five

David raised his eyebrows in mock innocence. "What?"

"Teasing her like that. If you're not interested in Cassy, don't lead her on. That's not like you at all—at least not the David I used to know."

Mrs. Dobranski came around the desk and faced him again. "I think by now you know how we feel about Cassy around here. Nothing would make us happier than to see the two of you get together. But I don't want to see her get hurt." She reached up to lay a hand on his shoulder, her serious eyes searching his. "You know what it's like to be hurt in love, David. Be careful, okay?"

David nodded, thoughtfully, and Mrs. Dobranski left the office. He walked behind the desk, sat back in the chair, and stretched his hands behind his head. Could Mrs. D. be right? He didn't want to get involved with Cassy, and yet he certainly was attracted to her. Taking off his shirt had been a reflex action—a normal reaction in the crisis. Still, he could have put his jacket on when they came in the office.

He reached across the desk to pick up his clipboard. Mrs. D. must be overreacting, he decided. Anyway, who did she think she was, telling him how to run his love life?

Yes, she was talking about love! He shook his head in amazement. He barely knew Cassy, and he certainly wasn't in love with her, or she with him. He hadn't done anything to lead her on. If she developed a crush on him, it was her own fault—not his!

He started flipping through the pages on his clipboard, not really seeing them. Finally, unable to concentrate, he laid it back down. Leaning forward, he steepled his hands and rested his chin on his fingertips. Why couldn't he get the image of Cassy's pretty face out of his mind?

He might as well go home, David decided. He certainly wasn't getting any work done here. He'd dismissed his last class when he'd heard Megan screaming. And he could just as easily finish working on his class plans for tomorrow at home. He stood up and stretched again, turning to look out the window. The office faced the road and the parking area in front of the barn. Most of the cars had gone by now, but Cassy's Honda was still there, near his Miata.

He heard light footsteps coming down the center aisle and glanced back at the doorway in time to see Cassy go past on her way out of the barn.

He sighed; it was time he headed home too. He crossed the few feet of office floor and snatched his jacket off the hook by the door. Slipping it on, he grabbed his clipboard and followed her.

Cassy was already seated in her car when David

emerged from the barn. He smiled and nodded as he went past, but went directly to his own car. After he'd started it, he glanced her way again, expecting to see her pulling out. Instead she appeared to be still trying to start the Honda. He waited, watching her for a few more minutes. Nothing seemed to be happening. He didn't hear any motor sounds except his own. He waited another minute, wondering if he should offer to help.

Cassy sat back, frustrated. Her battery was dead—again. She should have taken her dad's advice and bought a new one a month ago, when this happened the last time. Now she'd have to get someone to jump start it.

She glanced around. Mr. Dobranski hadn't come back yet. Mrs. Davis' car was still there, but she was still at the doctor's. Mrs. Dobranski might be able to help, but she was busy feeding the horses. That left David. Reluctantly, she looked in his direction. Not only was he still there, he was watching her. She hated to ask him for help, but. . . . She bit her lip and looked back at him.

When Cassy looked helplessly in his direction, David made his decision. He turned off the Miata and got out.

"Car trouble?" he asked, coming up beside her just as she opened her door.

"I'm afraid so. The battery is probably dead. My door wasn't shut all the way."

"I've got some jumper cables," he said. "But let me try starting it first."

Cassy was doing her best to keep from getting flustered. After all, he was just a man, doing what any other nice person would do under the circumstances.

She stepped aside and let him climb in and try to start the Honda. It refused to respond, just as it had a few minutes earlier.

"Okay, let's try those jumper cables," David said, climbing back out. He went to retrieve them from his car and pulled the Miata up in front of her Honda. Cassy opened the hood.

When he returned, it was hard to resist watching him as he leaned over to hook up the cables. Cassy stood back to observe his hands as they expertly attached the negative and positive clips. Even his hands were masculine—large and strong.

"Okay, start her up," he said, appearing not to notice the way she was watching him. Obediently, she climbed back in and turned the key. The engine purred to life. She smiled happily and waited while he unhooked the cables, then came to stand by her open car window. He leaned over and rested his elbows on the door.

"That should do it," he said, smiling into her eyes. "Just keep it running till you get home, and by that time it should be totally recharged."

"Thanks. I'm glad you were still here." She started to look away, intending to leave.

"Cassy. . . . "

She stopped and raised questioning eyes to meet his. Her heart was beating erratically at his proximity.

"I wanted to tell that you were great today . . . with Megan."

"Oh . . . thanks. You were a big help too. Guess we make a pretty good team."

"Yes, we do." His eyes looked sincerely into hers, melting her heart once again. She nodded, and after a moment he stepped back and away from her car. "See you tomorrow."

"Okay. 'Bye." She put the Honda in reverse and turned it around.

David watched as she pulled out, then climbed back in his own car and started it, smiling to himself. They *did* make a good team. If only she wasn't his student. . . .

The next day as Cassy was glancing over the bulletin board on her way out of the barn, she heard a news report coming from the TV in the office. It mentioned Community Hospital. Curious, she stepped into the open doorway and looked at the screen in time to hear the rest of the report. Her face went white as she learned that one of her favorite patients, a little girl waiting for a lung transplant, had just died.

"Oh, no!" She gasped in shock, her hand flying up to cover her mouth. She started to sink onto the office chair, her eyes filling with tears. She hadn't realized anyone else was there. But suddenly, as her knees went weak, she felt two strong arms come around her shoulders. She didn't protest when he turned her around to face him, and she saw through tear-misted eyes that it was David.

Gently he pulled her to his muscular chest. "Go ahead and cry," he told her, holding her to him and softly stroking her hair. "You're not working now— it's okay to show your grief."

Gratefully she nodded and allowed the pain to wash over her, wracking her body with tortured sobs. She was barely aware when he thrust his handkerchief into her hand, her fingers instinctively closing around it.

Self-consciously, she blew her nose into the soft cloth when she realized her tears were soaking his chest.

David cuddled her to him, enjoying the feel of her soft body next to his. The top of her head barely reached his chin, and he could smell the clean fresh scent of her shampoo. She felt so small and fragile.

Cassy wasn't aware of time passing as she stood wrapped in the comfort of his arms. Finally her tears were spent and she struggled to regain control. She allowed him to continue holding her rather than have him see her tear-swollen face. It was so reassuring to be consoled in his firm grasp.

He was the first to speak. "You shouldn't go home yet. Why don't you let me buy you dinner?"

Regretfully she pulled away from him. "Thanks, but I'm not exactly dressed for going out—and besides, I wouldn't be very good company." She stood facing him now, her red eyes lowered to the floor as she dabbed furiously at her nose with the handkerchief.

"All the more reason you shouldn't be alone," he insisted, taking her chin in his hand and tilting her head back, so she had to raise her tear-filled eyes to look into his deep blue ones. She melted at the tenderness she saw there.

"Let's go," he said, putting an arm around her shoulder and propelling her out the door before she could protest again.

"Mind if I drive your car?" he asked. When she said no, he took the keys from her before helping her into the passenger side and going around to the driver's seat.

They rode in silence toward the main highway. "How do burgers at your place sound?" he asked when he spotted a fast-food restaurant off the main road.

"Perfect," she admitted, glad to escape going into a restaurant. She gave him her order, and they went through the drive-thru window. Then she directed him to her apartment.

By the time they reached the complex, she had regained control of her emotions. She was almost able to forget why David had brought her home as she unlocked the door and stepped ahead of him into the living room.

"I like this," he remarked, looking around at the brightly decorated walls covered mostly with framed horse posters. They walked through to the dining area, and he began unpacking their burgers and laying them out on her small table. Cassy took two glasses out of the cabinet in the adjoining kitchen and a pitcher of iced tea from the refrigerator.

Over dinner he asked her to tell him about her patient. Since the initial shock of the child's death was over, Cassy was able to tell him all about what a sweet little girl she had been and how all the nurses had been rooting for her.

David listened sympathetically while she talked and took her hand when fresh tears threatened to escape the corners of her eyes.

After they'd finished eating, Cassy made coffee while David cleared the table of the wrappers from dinner, then seated himself on the red-and-gold Early American couch.

Cassy brought two mugs and set them on the coffee table before joining him on the sofa. He was leafing through one of the horse magazines displayed on the table. She noticed he stopped at an article about show jumping.

"Do you miss it?" she asked softly, tucking her

stockinged feet up under her on the couch and picking up her mug.

He took a deep breath and closed the book before laying it back on the coffee table. "Sometimes. I miss the excitement and the feeling of satisfaction I'd get after a good ride. And I miss Jet. I haven't been able to find another horse to match him." He picked up his mug and took a sip of the hot brew before continuing. "But I like what I do now. It isn't as exciting—but it's equally satisfying. And a heck of a lot safer." He smiled and turned to look at her.

Cassy was holding her mug while she listened. She returned his smile before taking another sip.

Still watching her, David continued. "I used to love all the traveling. But lately I find myself getting tired of the amount I still have to do. I'm seriously thinking about staying in this area. I feel comfortable here, since I lived nearby as a kid. At least I'll be doing another set of clinics after this one."

"That's great!" Cassy set down her mug. "When can I sign up?"

He put down his cup too, and turned back to her. "Actually, I was hoping you wouldn't," he said dryly.

The excited smile on her face faded. "You don't want me as a student?"

"No, I don't," he replied, looking into her wistful brown eyes. "I make it a policy never to get involved with my students."

"Oh. . . . " Cassy's heart started to beat erratically as she gazed into the darkening depths of David's eyes. The corner of his mouth turned up as he slowly reached behind her head and tilted her face toward his. She waited breathlessly for the kiss she knew was coming. When at last his lips touched hers, it was with a tender passion, as though he was afraid of hurting her. She responded with an intensity she'd never known before. Her arms encircled him as he deepened the kiss.

But then suddenly he drew back.

Puzzled, she watched him sit up and pivot away.

He stood, raking his hands through his dark curls, searching for the right words. Finally he turned back to face her. "I think I'd better go. You're still my student for two more weeks, and I don't take advantage of the women I teach, no matter how attracted I am to them. You had a shock tonight and needed someone. I want to be sure when I kiss you that it's me you want and not a need for comfort."

He walked toward the kitchen and asked over his shoulder, "Will you be okay if I have Mr. D. pick me up now?"

It was an effort, but Cassy managed to keep the rejection she was feeling out of her voice. "Sure." She picked up their cups and followed him to the kitchen.

While David used the phone, she poured more coffee. They sat at the table with their cups, making small talk while they waited for Mr. Dobranski.

"I'll see you in class on Saturday," David said when the headlights approached. He rose to go, but hesitated a moment at her bereft expression. Taking her chin in his hand once again, he kissed her soundly on her lips. "Only two more weeks," he said solemnly and went out the door.

The next two weeks passed slowly for Cassy. After David had left the night he'd kissed her, she'd sat at her table for a long time drinking coffee while she tried to decide what to do.

She'd always wanted to be a good rider. No, a *great* rider. But as a girl she'd never had the chance to learn. Now, as an adult, she was making her dream come true. David was an excellent teacher. She knew she wouldn't have made the progress she had in the last two months without his clinic. If she continued to take his classes, she could do even better. Did she really want to give up the opportunity?

Her lips had curled up in a smile when she remembered the feel of his lips on hers. Even if he agreed to date her if she remained his student, she knew it wouldn't work. She wouldn't be able to concentrate on her riding.

Besides, she'd reasoned, she was growing to like David more all the time. Even though she knew a lasting relationship probably wouldn't be possible since he'd be leaving again in a few months, she didn't want to miss the chance to get to know him better in the time they had left.

There were other instructors who could teach her to ride. But it had been a long time since she'd met a man who sent her pulse racing the way David did.

Finally, exhausted, she'd gone to bed after deciding to put off signing up for another clinic. She still spent most of her free time at the stable and frequently ran into David.

He never suggested seeing her away from work, but there was a new intimacy between them. If there was no one else nearby, he'd stop to talk to her about how her life was going. When anyone else was around, he kept their conversation limited to the subject of riding.

Finally, the day of her last class with David arrived. Cassy had still not registered for his next clinic session. To the few people who'd asked, she'd simply said she couldn't get off work that many weeks in a row—which was true. No one except David knew the real reason was that she would no longer be considered his student, and they would be free to begin a new, equal relationship.

Even so, she had mixed feelings going into the last clinic. David had been a very good teacher, and she knew her riding had improved a great deal as a result of his clinic. Although she'd known most of the people in her class before they began the clinic, they all had developed a special camaraderie by learning and suffering together over the last two months. Cassy knew she would miss the classes.

David began the last lesson by reminding them of their early mistakes and reviewing all the exercises and special tricks he had taught them. Finally, as he said good-bye individually, he presented each rider with a certificate and shook their hands before they left the ring.

Cassy managed to arrange to be last in line. He approached her the same as all the others, still holding one certificate.

"Well, Cassy, you made it," he said, a twinkle in his eye. "You've come a long way in two months. You should be very proud of yourself, and I hope you will continue to take lessons . . . with someone else. And now—" He handed her the certificate. "—you are officially graduated from my class—and no longer my student."

"Thank goodness," Cassy teased, shaking his hand and taking the diploma.

He arched an eyebrow. "I hope you mean because now we're free to see each other, and not because of my lessons."

She tried to keep a straight face. "Well, actually. . . . " Suddenly she smiled. "Yes, I'd love to see you outside of work."

"Good." He returned her smile. "Would you like to take a trail ride tomorrow? I have the whole day off."

"Sure. I'm off too. I usually come out after church— about eleven. I could pack a lunch for a picnic by the lake."

"That sounds great. I'll pick you up at eleven-thirty. Now I think we'd better head back to the barn before everyone starts wondering if I flunked you."

Together they walked out of the arena. Outside the gate Cassy dismounted and led General back to his stall while David headed back to the office. She finished taking care of General, and by the time she left, David was back in the ring giving the final lesson to his advanced class.

The next day began like a typical Sunday for Cassy. On weekends when she didn't go home to see her parents, she usually attended a small church near her apartment. After the service, she returned home and changed into a pair of snug jeans and a pullover sweater and began packing a lunch in a leather pouch to attach to her saddle. By the time she saw David's car pulling into the driveway, all she had to do was pull on her Western riding boots and grab her light jacket. She let her hair hang free to her shoulders with just a headband pulling it away from her face.

It was a beautiful crisp day—perfect for riding. Cassy was locking her apartment door as David pulled up next to it, so he waited without turning off the ignition. Today the top was down on his convertible, so Cassy tossed her things in the back and hopped in without opening the door.

"I've always wanted to do that." She beamed him a proud smile.

He gave a low chuckle as he shifted into reverse. She noticed that today he too was dressed casually in jeans and boots with a blue Western shirt. His normally well-combed black curls were obviously windblown, giving him a totally different look from the stern riding instructor she was used to.

They chatted casually about current events, and before she knew it, they were pulling up to Greenwood. They took their jackets and Cassy's saddlebags from behind the seats.

"Don't you think you should put the top up?" Cassy asked as they started to walk away.

David looked up at the clear sky and raised his eyebrows.

Cassy laughed. "Have you already forgotten what Florida weather is like?"

"You're right. Liquid sunshine." He raised the top of the Miata. "Just in case," he said with a wink.

They walked together to the tack room to check out a pair of Western saddles. David had arranged to borrow a large and very spirited thoroughbred mare named Josephine who belonged to the Dobranskis. He and Cassy parted long enough to tack up their horses and met again outside the barn to mount up and head out on the trail.

The beginning of the path through the woods was narrow so David rode ahead on Josephine until it widened enough for Cassy to come up next to him.

Riding behind, she admired how good he looked in the saddle. The whole time she was taking his lessons she had never actually seen him ride. Now she saw that he was completely at home on a horse. Although Josephine was a high-spirited mare and often shied at nothing at all when even the most advanced students rode her, David seemed to have total control. The mare walked placidly along as though she had complete confidence in her rider.

General, on the other hand, seemed to be sensing Cassy's own nervous energy and was prancing along like a young colt. Cassy found she needed to concentrate on keeping him under control.

They reached a wider part of the trail. David pulled up the mare and waited for General to come alongside. "Relax," he said, noting the gelding's behavior. "Take some deep breaths and keep your respirations even. A horse can tell when its rider is uneasy. Then he gets nervous too. If he feels you breathing normally, he thinks everything is under control and he calms down." He started to walk out again while Cassy and General walked next to them.

Within a few moments, Cassy could feel the difference in her horse. She smiled at David. "You were right—but now he wants to go to sleep on me."

"Then let's wake him up. Are you ready to canter?" He nodded ahead at the open field they were approaching.

"Sure. Race you!" Cassy cued General, and he instantly sprang into a gallop. There wasn't time to think of anything but staying aboard as they bounded through the meadow, jumping over logs on the ground and dodging the few scattered trees they encountered. Cassy could hear the pounding hoofbeats of David's horse as first they fell into a canter behind her, quickly came even with General, and then pulled ahead. General seemed to be enjoying the exhilarating ride as much as his rider so she gave him his head and he gave her a valiant effort. Cassy knew Josephine was a faster horse so she wasn't surprised when General fell behind. The race itself was reward enough, and by the time they reached the other side of the clearing, her cheeks were flushed with excitement and pleasure.

"Does this path still go to the pond?" David asked, turning triumphantly to look at her when he reached a fork in the dirt road.

"Yes, it goes all the way around and comes out on the other path. There's a perfect spot to picnic near the water."

"Okay—let's go." They began walking single file again, carefully picking their way around holes where rainwater had washed away the sand as the path began to slope downward toward the pond. They rode silently now, enjoying the peace of the woods around them. The only noises were the slight breeze through the trees and the birds calling to one another. Occasionally a rabbit or field mouse made a rustling sound in the bushes as it scurried out of their path.

As they came out of the trees and in sight of the water, David stopped and put his finger to his lips to warn her to be quiet. She followed his eyes and almost gasped in delight. A deer was standing by the pond, drinking. Silently they watched until it noticed them. Even then, it didn't appear frightened, but gazed at them with huge brown eyes for a moment before bounding off into the brush.

"Wasn't that the most beautiful thing you've ever seen?" Cassy sighed. "I wish I had a camera."

"Yeah. I've noticed before that when you're on a

horse, other animals don't seem to notice you. It's almost like being invisible.''

They walked their horses on out of the woods toward the pond, which everyone called "the lake." There they dismounted and tied the horses in the shade of a large oak tree near the water.

While Cassy unpacked the sandwiches and a thermos of hot chocolate, David spread out a Western blanket on the grass.

"Have you ever been here before?" Cassy asked. She handed him a cup and filled it as he answered.

"Not for a long time. Sometimes a group of us kids would go riding and then have a picnic here. We used to skinny-dip till Mr. D. caught us." He chuckled. "I think he would have joined us if he thought he could get away with it."

Cassy smiled. "You must have been a mischievous little boy." She poured her own cocoa into the thermos top and sat cross-legged on the grass.

He sat down across from her. "Some people think I still am. In fact, I think I'd still enjoy shedding my clothes and taking a swim. Care to join me?"

She laughed at the devilish look he was giving her. "Not in this weather!" She pulled her jacket closer around her to emphasize the point.

"Yeah, I guess you're right. Besides, I'd probably get fired if some other trail riders caught us." He smiled agreeably and reached for a sandwich.

"I love it here. You can forget all about the rest of the world." Cassy unwrapped her sandwich and took a bite.

"I'd forgotten how peaceful it is." He stared pensively out at the water. "You really *could* forget everything.'' He started to munch on a sandwich. ''Hey, this is good. I didn't know you could cook,'' he teased.

''Well, I'd hardly call putting together a submarine sandwich 'cooking', but yeah, I know my way around a kitchen. How about you? Do you like to cook?'' She took another bite.

''Sometimes. I like to prepare full meals for company, but I get tired of cooking for myself.'' He finished his sandwich and crumpled up the wrapper, stuffing it back in the leather pouch. ''I'll have to make you my famous beef Burgundy; it's almost as good as my mom's.''

''I'd like that. Is it her recipe?''

''Yeah. I have a sister, but she never liked to cook, so Mom taught me.'' He stretched out on his side and lazily reached for the bag of chocolate-chip cookies Cassy had left in the center of the blanket.

''Where does your family live now?'' Cassy asked. She had finished her sandwich too, and extended her legs to reach a semi-reclining position facing him.

''Mostly in Texas. We moved there when I was in high school. My sister got married and moved to another town only forty minutes away. She has a couple of kids and my folks love to spoil them. Look!''

Cassy followed his arm pointing at the water, and saw a pair of mallard ducks swimming across the smooth surface of the pond. They watched delightedly as the two birds bobbed under the water repeatedly, looking for things to eat. Sometimes their tails stuck straight up in the air, making an amusing sight. When the ducks reached the shore, they waddled up on the sand, their bright orange feet in sharp contrast to the muted browns of the female and the bright green, almost iridescent, head of the male. They wandered toward Cassy and David, cocking their heads as though curious about these strange visitors to their pond.

"I wonder if they like cookies," David said, breaking one in several pieces and tossing it toward them. The crumbs landed near the ducks' feet, but they merely tilted their heads to look at them before waddling away in search of something better.

"I guess they don't like my cookies." Cassy laughed. "Oh, well, that leaves more for us!" She took one and bit voraciously into it. "Mmm . . . they don't know what they're missing." She glanced at David and found him watching her with an intense look. Her eyes locked with his, and she felt her pulse quicken.

He reached over and brushed the crumbs away from the corner of her mouth with his thumb.

Still gazing into his eyes, she put down the rest of the cookie and tossed the bag out of the way, suddenly hungry for his kiss.

Chapter Six

David's hand moved from the edge of her mouth to trace the full curves of her lips, then slowly to the back of her neck to draw her toward him.

She allowed him to pull her into his arms, her own going instinctively around his neck. She could feel the strong, fast beat of his heart through the cotton material of his shirt.

Now his mouth was leaving hers to trail tiny wonderful kisses down her face and neck. Cassy forgot everything as she lost herself in his warm embrace.

Suddenly a welcoming whinny from General alerted them to the approach of other horses. Freezing in position for a moment, they listened and could hear voices mingled with the advancing hoofbeats.

Their eyes met in an intimate gaze, and Cassy smiled apologetically.

David muttered something about "lack of privacy" under his breath, and they quickly sat up and repaired their hair and clothing. By the time the riders emerged from the woods, Cassy had retrieved the bag of cookies, and David was helping her finish them off. Both tried to appear to be talking casually.

Cassy waved as she recognized Wendy in front, followed by two other women from Greenwood, also students of David's. The trio walked their horses toward the pond and the two picnickers.

"Hi. It's a perfect day for riding, isn't it?" Wendy was the first to get within hearing distance. Her mischievous eyes took in the entire scene before her. "It looks like you two are having a great time. Did you save any food for us?"

Cassy obligingly held out the bag, which only had one cookie left.

"Thanks, but I'll pass. You guys have fun." Wendy gave Cassy a knowing look as she turned her horse back toward the path. The other two riders fell in behind her and they all waved and continued on the path around the pond.

David met Cassy's eyes with such a disappointed expression that she couldn't help smiling.

"What?" he asked, not amused with the situation himself.

"You look just like a little boy who's had his lollipop taken away!" she answered, laughing.

He continued to look at her pensively for a moment, then smiled grimly, fully aware that they would still be in partial view of the riders as they circled the pond. "I think I'll get my contribution to the picnic," he said, standing up.

Cassy admired his lean physique as he walked casually back to Josephine and produced a jug of wine from his saddlebag.

She finished the last of her hot chocolate before he returned, then held up her cup expectantly.

Somberly he uncorked the jug and poured them each a cup, then lounged back on the blanket facing her.

They drank silently, enjoying the peace and beauty of their surroundings and trying to ignore the physical attraction they both knew was there.

When he'd finished his second refill, David placed the empty cup by the jug on the blanket and turned over to his back, using his hands for a pillow. He gave Cassy a lazy smile. ''That was great. Now I'm ready for a nap.'' He closed his eyes and appeared to fall asleep instantly.

The wine was having the same drowsy effect on Cassy. She placed her empty cup next to his and stretched out on her end of the blanket.

Sleep did not come so quickly for her, though. She was still all too aware of his very masculine presence resting only inches away. While she longed to feel his kisses again, she knew it was too soon to get so serious.

Did David feel as strongly for her as she did for him? Though they'd known each other for two months, they hadn't started dating until today. She wondered if she knew the real David.

She raised up on one elbow and looked at him. He reminded her again of a little boy—so innocent as he slept peacefully. But, she reminded herself, he was also dangerously charming with all the women he came in contact with. She wasn't the only one who found him attractive.

She looked at him tenderly. This could be the man she'd been waiting to give her heart to. If she did, would he break it in two? He'd been married once—unsuccessfully. How could she know if he'd want to risk commitment again? And if he did, would it mean as much to him as to her?

Cassy picked up a twig and absently chewed it as painful memories began to flood over her. Her boyfriend in high school had told her he loved her. She'd believed him too—until her friends had revealed the lies that he was telling his friends boasting about his sexual prowess with her. When she tearfully told him good-bye, he'd wasted no time finding someone new.

As a nursing student, she'd been so flattered when a handsome young intern had shown an interest in her. By their second date, she was sure she was in love. Like her first boyfriend, he'd told her he loved her. But with two more years of internship and then a residency still ahead of him he wasn't ready for marriage. As soon as he realized she wanted commitment, he ran the other way.

Cassy tossed the twig away and sat up, hugging her knees. The hardest lesson had been Bill, the father of one of her patients. He was kind and thoughtful, and she'd believed him when he'd said his marriage was over. He'd convinced her he loved her. She got off work early one night to surprise him. But she was the one who was surprised, when she arrived at his home to find his wife there. Even now, Cassy's cheeks burned at the memory of her anger and humiliation. Never again would she allow herself to completely trust a man that way.

She sighed and settled back down on the blanket, feeling more and more drowsy. Slowly she drifted off to sleep. . . .

"Cassy, wake up," David called her softly.

Regretfully, she slowly opened her eyes and looked sleepily into David's. She was surprised to find her head resting comfortably on his shoulder, her outside arm stretched across his chest.

"I'm afraid we need to head back—now." Carefully he removed her arm and slipped out from under her to sit up.

It took a few minutes for her still-sleepy eyes to take in the change in weather. The sun had completely disappeared, and dark clouds were rapidly moving in. David quickly jumped to his feet and began to gather up the remnants of their picnic.

As soon as she realized what was happening, Cassy shook her head to clear it and began to help him. Within minutes they'd repacked everything and were ready to leave.

She understood as well as David did the danger of being out on horseback in a storm. Florida lightning could be deadly, and a horse's high body temperature could attract it. They needed to get back to shelter as quickly as possible.

Without waiting for a leg up, Cassy quickly mounted. She glanced at David, who was gathering his reins.

"Let's go," he said.

They began to walk back the way they'd come, as quickly as was safe on the upward-sloping path. As soon as they reached the top, they began a trot and then allowed the horses to gallop through the field. This time they were too intent on getting back quickly to enjoy the view. So far they hadn't heard any thunder, but the rain was already beginning. By the time they slowed to a walk for the last stretch of path, both horses and riders were soaked to the skin.

They took their horses directly to their respective stalls and untacked them. Cassy was grateful to find that someone had already cleaned the stalls. But they still needed to give the horses a good grooming and rub them dry. When Cassy finished, she put away her things in the tack room and followed the sound of voices to the office. She found David there leaning on the front of the desk and holding the phone, listening. He nodded to her and motioned for her to come in.

Mr. Dobranski was sitting at the desk. "A little wet out there, huh?" He grinned, noting her still-wet clothing. She could see through the window behind him that by now the rain was coming down in buckets. He gestured toward the full pot of coffee in the corner. "Looks like you could use some warming up."

"Sure could." Cassy walked across to the table to take one of the Styrofoam cups and help herself to some coffee. David and Mr. D. already each had a cup in front of them.

"How soon can the vet come?" David said into the phone. "Uh-huh. Okay, I'll be there in half an hour. Don't worry, she'll be okay."

He hung up and turned to Mr. Dobranski. "I'd better take Cassy home. It sounds like Maggie could use some moral support. One of her horses slipped on the wet grass and slid into the fence. It probably isn't too bad but will need stitches, and it may take a while." He glanced out the window. "The rain is letting up a little. Maybe we can make a run for it." He quickly drained his cup and tossed it in the trash can. "May we borrow an umbrella?"

"Sure." The older man produced one from under the desk. "Let Cassy finish her coffee, though. She looks chilled to the bone."

David turned back to her and noticed that she did indeed seem to be trembling from the cold.

She was huddled over her coffee cup, holding it in both hands as she tried to absorb its warmth.

He immediately stepped over to her and took the cup. "Take off that wet jacket," he ordered.

Obediently, she peeled off the soaked jacket and handed it to Mr. Dobranski, who produced a large towel from the bathroom and handed it to David. Muttering something about needing to check the horses, he made a quick exit.

Cassy glanced up quickly at David's sudden intake of breath when he stepped in front of her and got a glimpse of her, with droplets of rain glistening in her hair and her sweater clinging to her curves. There was no doubt she saw desire in the darkening pupils of his eyes.

But just as quickly as the passion had emerged, he restrained it. A shadow came over his face as he concentrated on rubbing her arms and shoulders with the towel.

"Are you okay?" he asked.

"Yeah. At least I will be once I get home and into some dry clothes."

She returned the wet towel to the bathroom. "Thanks. Now we'd better get going."

David put his arm around her shoulders and ushered her to the door, where he opened the umbrella and held it over both of them until they reached his car.

"I'm glad I thought to put the top up," he said, winking as he helped her into the driver's seat. The rain had slowed to a light drizzle.

She moved over to the passenger side, so he could climb in behind her. He started the ignition, and they fastened their seat belts. As the heat came on, Cassy gradually warmed up and stopped shivering.

"Would you like me to go with you?" she asked when they pulled onto the main road. "Maybe I could help."

David kept his eyes on the wet road. "Thanks—but

the vet is on his way. He'll probably tranquilize the mare while he sews her up. I think we can handle it. You should go take a nice hot bath and relax." He chuckled. "This reminds me of the day we met— except this time you're just plain wet."

Cassy grimaced. "I must have made quite an impression."

"Actually, you did. I couldn't understand how a kid like you could be so attractive all covered with mud. I thought you were much too young for me and I needed to keep my distance. It was darn hard to stay professional with you in my class." He stopped at a light and took his eyes momentarily off the road to meet hers.

Suddenly Cassy felt warm in spite of her wet clothing. How did he do this to her? She met his gaze till the light changed and he moved his eyes to the road. She looked out at the dismal weather, but her heart felt sunny and warm.

They rode on in silence until they reached her apartment. The rain had ceased by then so she told him to keep the umbrella in case he needed it at Maggie's. He stopped the car and she turned toward him. He took her in his arms and kissed her briefly.

"I'll call you," he promised as she climbed out.

At the door, she turned to wave, but he was already pulling away, his eyes on the road.

Cassy took David's advice and relaxed in a hot bubble bath. Her thoughts naturally turned back to him as she soaked. What would have happened if the other riders hadn't come along? She had no doubt that he had desired her. But was it more than just physical? Did he care for her as she did for him? How *did* she feel about him?

At first she'd thought he was arrogant and aloof, but she'd found him attractive anyway. Then she'd seen the other side of him when he'd taught the children's class, and later when he'd been so sympathetic when her little patient died.

Today had been even more of an eye-opener. She'd seen him as he must be with other women, those who were not his students. She'd liked him even more. Enough to fall in love with him?

She sighed and regretfully pulled the plug in the tub. She'd better get out and dress. She hoped David would be calling soon.

As if on cue, the phone rang. Quickly she stepped out and wrapped a towel around herself before running to pick up before the answering machine started to click on. She turned off the machine and lifted the receiver.

"Hello? Oh, hi, Mom. Yes, I'm okay. I just got out of the tub."

The familiar voice on the other end sounded worried. "I called several times today. Didn't you get my messages?"

"Sorry. I went riding after church and forgot to check my machine when I came in. Is anything wrong?"

"Oh, no, I just wanted to make sure you were coming for Thanksgiving. It's this Thursday, you know."

"Sure." Cassy stretched the phone cord as far as it would go, barely reaching her robe on the hook behind the bedroom door. "I'm working, though, so I can't come till after my shift." She tucked the phone under her chin and slipped into her long blue kimono.

"That's okay; we'll have a late dinner. Would you like to bring anyone?" her mom asked hopefully.

Cassy hadn't thought of that. "Well, maybe. I *have* met someone . . . let me ask if he has plans."

"He? You have a new boyfriend?" She sounded excited.

"Don't go planning the wedding yet, Mom. We've just had our first date," Cassy answered patiently. "But I'd better get off the phone 'cause I'm expecting his call. Would you like me to bring the pies again?"

"Please. Can you be here by five?"

"I think so. Are Ben and Joyce coming?"

"Of course. And Janet and the kids. We'll look forward to seeing you."

"Me too. See you Thursday then. 'Bye, Mom." Cassy placed the receiver back on the cradle and returned to the bathroom to finish dressing for bed, listening for the phone the whole time.

Finally, clad in her cotton nightgown and the kimono and feeling deliciously clean, she suddenly realized the hunger pangs she was feeling were getting stronger. She glanced at the clock. Eight o'clock—no wonder she was famished!

She headed to the kitchen and opened the refrigerator hopefully. No leftovers. She'd have to go shopping tomorrow. She decided to make a sandwich, since she still had some ham and cheese left from making the subs this morning. Had it been only this morning? She spread the bread thickly with mayonnaise. She glanced at the clock again. She closed the sandwich and poured herself a tall glass of milk, then carried both to the table and set them down before continuing to the TV in the corner and turning it on. Idly she flicked the channels until she found a situation comedy. By the time she finished eating, the phone had still not rung.

Cassy glared at it as she carried her dishes to the sink to rinse and put in the dishwasher.

The comedy ended, and she flicked channels again. Unable to find anything that interested her, she switched off the TV and picked up a paperback mystery she was halfway through. It was good reading, so she became engrossed in the story and was able to temporarily forget about waiting for David to call.

Several hours later when Cassy finished the book and set it back on the table, she was surprised to realize how late it was. Thinking back, she tried to remember if David had said when he'd call. Maybe he didn't mean tonight after all. She knew she'd have to be up early for work, and now she was tired. Sensibly she decided to go to bed.

David threw his jacket on the couch and sank wearily onto his armchair. It had been a long night. The vet had taken longer than he'd expected to sew up Maggie's mare. He was glad he'd gone, though. Poor Maggie was really shaken up. It would have been nice to have Cassy there too, but she would definitely have been a distraction. He still couldn't get the memory of the feel of her in his arms out of his mind. It was probably a good thing they'd been interrupted that afternoon—things were getting serious. But she wasn't the kind of woman who took a relationship lightly. He might be leaving in a few weeks, and where would that leave her?

Still . . . he might decide to stay. She was certainly worth seeing again. They'd just have to take it slowly. He glanced at the clock. It was too late to call her now. She'd probably gone to bed hours ago since she had to be at work by seven. He'd try to catch her at Greenwood tomorrow.

Right now he'd better try to catch a few hours of sleep himself.

The next day at work was especially hectic for Cassy. A new strain of flu was going around, and several children were admitted with dehydration and other complications. They were short-staffed as well, since an aide and two nurses had called in sick with the same bug. Cassy was kept busy signing off admission orders and starting IV's. There was so much to do that she had to save most of her charting till after the evening shift had come on and received her report, when they could take over the rest of her duties.

Cassy gave an exhausted sigh of relief as she signed off the last chart and hung it back on the rack. She was already an hour into overtime. That meant she would hit the rush-hour congestion going home. Oh, well, she'd do her shopping on the way. Maybe some of the traffic would clear by then.

She said good-bye to the staff in the nurses' station as she retrieved her purse from the medicine room in back and headed for the elevator.

Since it was past the usual shift change time, she didn't have long to wait for an elevator and was able to quickly punch her time card and be on her way.

The parking lot was half empty, since most of the day shift had left and the evening staff wasn't as large. Cassy had no trouble finding her car.

As she'd expected, the traffic was moving at a snail's pace. Cassy was grateful her favorite grocery was nearby and she gladly pulled off the highway into the parking lot.

The store too was crowded with after-work shoppers and it took her another hour to buy her week's worth of groceries and ingredients for the Thanksgiving pies and get through the checkout line.

Finally she reached her apartment. She carried the first bag of groceries with her while she unlocked the door. As she set it on the counter, she glanced eagerly at her phone machine. Darn! She must have forgotten to turn it back on after her mother's call last night! What if David had called?

Angry at herself for not remembering to leave it on, she trudged back to the car for the other two bags of food. As she approached her apartment door, she heard the jangle of the phone. She rushed to answer it, only to hear a click at the other end when she picked it up.

Oh, no! That was probably David, she chided herself. Should she try to call him back? But she didn't know where he was. And what if it was someone else?

Cassy looked at the clock. She'd better get out to the stable and take care of General. Maybe David was there too.

Quickly she put away her frozen and refrigerated groceries and changed into her jeans and sweater.

Luckily by now the traffic wasn't too bad, and she made good time. Still, it was six o'clock by the time she pulled up to the barn. Disappointed, she noticed that David's car was not there. Of course he usually finished his classes by five-thirty. She parked and went on into the barn anyway.

It was almost deserted, since most of the owners had already come and gone. Outside it was almost dark and the barn lights were on. Cassy spotted Mr. Dobranski and headed toward him. He was going down the aisle flinging hay into each stall.

"Well, hi," he said, barely glancing at her as he continued down the row. "General's all taken care of.

He was getting pretty upset about everybody else getting dinner first, so I fed him.''

"I'm sorry," Cassy apologized. "I had to work late. Can I do anything?''

"We figured it was something like that." The older man threw in the last of the hay and turned toward the office.

"Everything's done, and I'm about to call it a night." He chuckled and turned back to her with a twinkle in his eye. "Of course, General might appreciate a good grooming 'cause he rolled in the mud in the pasture today.''

"Oh, no!" Cassy groaned as she looked in on her horse and saw that Mr. D. was right. It didn't seem to be bothering General at all as he contentedly munched his hay. But he had obviously had a great time in the aftermath of yesterday's rain. His beautiful brown coat was caked with mud.

"Okay." Cassy sighed. "Looks like I've got my work cut out for me." She assembled her grooming equipment and started the time-consuming job of cleaning him up. Although tedious, the work wasn't hard, and it helped relieve some of the stress of the day. The time passed quickly.

As she put the brushes back in her grooming kit, Cassy glared at General. "You'd better not try that again." She patted him anyway just to show there were no hard feelings. "See you tomorrow—hopefully on time," she told him and strolled back to the tack room to put away her things.

This time she had remembered to put the answering machine on, and the red light was blinking when she came in. Eagerly, she pressed the button to retrieve the message.

"Hi," said the voice she was waiting for. "This is David. I was hoping to see you at Greenwood. Maggie's horse is okay. Maybe I'll see you tomorrow. 'Bye."

That was it? He didn't want her to call him back? Maybe he wasn't home. Disappointed, she finished putting away the rest of the nonperishable groceries she'd left on the counter earlier in her haste to get to the stable. Then she fixed herself a frozen dinner and ate alone in front of the TV again. The phone remained frustratingly silent. After eating and cleaning up, she took a shower and went to bed.

The next morning Cassy made sure she remembered to leave her answering machine on before leaving for work. It was another busy day and she had to stay late again to finish up paperwork.

This time, since her shopping was done, she fought the traffic and went straight to Greenwood. She looked hopefully for David's little red car, but noted with disappointment that it wasn't there. She parked anyway, and taking her change of clothes with her, headed for the office.

Mr. Dobranski was coming out as she reached the doorway and she almost bumped into him. Stepping back to allow him to come out, she smiled apologetically. "Sorry, I'm running late again."

"That's okay." He seemed in no hurry. "General is still out in the pasture. It's pretty well dried out, so he should be in better shape today even if he rolled again." He grinned and stepped around her.

"That's good. I'd hate to have to give him a bath before it warms up." Cassy started into the office and saw it was empty. She turned back to Mr. Dobranski, who continued walking down the aisle. "Is David coming out today?" she asked hopefully.

"No," he said over his shoulder, "he went out to the Grand Cypress. I think he's doing some seminars out at the Equestrian Center there. He probably won't be back here till his class tomorrow evening." Mr. Dobranski picked up a manure rake and headed into an empty stall.

"Oh." David hadn't mentioned that. Of course, she hadn't talked to him since Sunday evening, and now it was Tuesday night. She'd better talk to him tonight if she was going to invite him for Thanksgiving. She went ahead and changed into casual clothes and finished up her barn chores.

Cassy was exhausted by the time she trudged up the walk to her apartment and unlocked her door. She shrugged off her jacket and threw it on the couch along with her work clothes. Her mood improved a little when she saw the red light blinking on her machine. But it crashed back down when she listened to the message and heard it was just her mother wanting to know if she was bringing her guest for Thanksgiving.

She began fixing another frozen dinner while she debated with herself over whether to try calling him. She'd have to call her mother back either way. Finally she decided to try to reach him.

Somewhat nervously, she dialed the number he'd given her for his trailer and listened as it rang again and again. Should she try calling at Maggie's? He'd told her she could leave a message there if he wasn't home. At least Maggie might know what his plans were. She finally decided to try there and dialed Maggie's number. It only rang twice.

"Pine Haven," said the familiar deep voice.

"David?" She hadn't expected him to answer the phone.

"Yeah, hi, Cassy!" He sounded pleased. "Guess we keep missing each other. How are you?"

"Busy. We've been swamped with flu victims at work, so I've had to work late. I heard you were out at the Grand Cypress. How'd it go?"

"Great. It's quite a place. They'll be hosting some show jumping events next year, and they asked me to officiate. I may even help design the course, which would be very challenging."

Cassy's heart leapt with joy. That meant he'd have to come back! "That's great," she said, trying not to sound too excited.

"I'm thinking more and more about staying in this area," David continued. "Central Florida seems to be growing fast and the horse industry with it. There should be plenty of work for me here. The hard part will be finding the time to do it all!"

"Well, that's encouraging." Cassy paused, wondering if he'd still have time for her. Should she ask him about Thanksgiving or wait to see if he brought it up?

"I'm afraid I don't have much free time the rest of the week," David said, as though reading her thoughts. "Because of the holiday, I'm doing my usual Thursday lessons tomorrow and Friday. This will be a tough holiday for Maggie, so I'm spending Thanksgiving Day here. Then Saturday I'll have my usual classes at Greenwood and Pine Haven and Sunday I'll be back at Grand Cypress for a meeting to work out the details for some clinics."

"Oh. . . . Well, I'm going to be pretty busy too." She hoped her disappointment didn't show in her voice. "I'm working through Friday, but maybe I'll see you at Greenwood between classes." She paused, hoping he'd ask about her holiday plans.

"Okay." He sounded preoccupied. "Maggie has dinner ready so I'd better go. Maybe I'll see you tomorrow."

" 'Bye." Cassy set the phone back down with an angry click. He didn't even ask if *she* had plans for dinner on Thursday. He just wanted to make sure Maggie wasn't alone! Hurt and frustrated, she decided to take her shower before calling her mother.

As she let the warm water beat on her face and body, her thoughts kept turning back to David. Was she being unrealistic hoping for a serious relationship with him? Surely he had any number of women to choose from. Maybe he liked playing the field. If he wasn't ready to commit to one woman, did she really want to share him?

Cassy reached for the soap as her thoughts turned to another problem in the relationship. He was certainly close to Maggie. They'd been friends a long time. Was it just friendship now and a sense of responsibility that made him want to take care of his friend's widow? Or could there be a new romance developing? Maggie was very attractive, and David certainly was too. Living so close together, wasn't it likely that romance could evolve? She'd felt a real pang of jealousy when David said he was spending Thanksgiving with Maggie, and again when he cut off his conversation with her to have dinner with the brunette tonight. Right now they were eating together, alone in Maggie's house. What if one thing led to another. . . .

No! Cassy determinedly shook her head and began to scrub her body, trying to rid her mind of the negative thoughts while she washed away the dirt. She was being selfish wishing David would spend the holiday with her. After all, Maggie had just lost her husband!

Cassy finished washing and rinsed herself, wishing

all the doubts would wash away as easily. She dried and dressed for bed before calling her mother and explaining that her friend already had plans.

The next day at work she had little time to think about anything but her job. Another nurse had come down with the flu, leaving them even more short-handed. Luckily the patient census was low because the doctors tried to send as many home for the holiday as possible. There wouldn't be any routine or non-emergency surgery for the same reason. But, with so many discharges, there was plenty of paperwork to finish before Cassy could leave. At least the next few days should be quiet.

She drove directly to Greenwood again and was glad to see David's car there. She caught a glimpse of him in the arena, apparently teaching one of his usual Thursday classes.

Still wearing her nursing uniform, she strode on in to the office bathroom to change to jeans, then cleaned her horse's vacant stall.

David's class was still in progress, so she took General's halter from the tack room, along with a handful of feed to bribe him, and headed for the pasture.

General was happily grazing and didn't even look up till she whistled. When he looked her way she held out her hand enticingly so he could smell the grain. Obligingly, he trotted over and reached for the feed, and Cassy slipped the red halter over his head.

He didn't resist as she led him back to the barn and his clean stall. Since it was almost feeding time, Cassy knew there wouldn't be time to ride, but she had time to groom him. At least he hadn't repeated his trick of rolling in the mud.

David's class was apparently over, and the barn was crowded with horses and riders coming and going. Cassy didn't see David but knew he'd see her car before he could leave.

She decided to let him find her if he was interested and assembled what she needed to groom her horse. Intent on her work and lost in her own thoughts, she didn't notice that the barn was gradually emptying as everyone finished their chores and went on their way. By the time she finished brushing, there were only a few people left.

General was beginning to get restless and resisted having to stand still for her as he smelled the feed and heard it being poured into his stallmates' buckets. He began pawing the sawdust in his floor impatiently.

"Okay, I get the message." Cassy laughed. "Dinner coming right up." She deposited the last brush in her tote box and turned to head to the tack room. Out of habit, she glanced in his water bucket to make sure it was full, and gasped in horror when she saw a furry brown body floating in the water.

"What's wrong?" David asked, poking his head in just then.

"T-there's something in his bucket." She pointed, stepping back and as far away from the bucket as she could get in the stall.

Frowning, David slid the stall door open just enough to slip inside and peeked into the bucket. Then he laughed as he picked up the drowned mouse by the tail and held it up to show her.

"It's okay," he said, obviously amused. "It's dead."

"Please, just get it out of here." Cassy shuddered.

David grinned and obligingly left the stall, still holding the small corpse by the tail. Cassy emptied the water bucket and washed it thoroughly before putting it back and refilling it. David still hadn't returned, so Cassy began to scoop out General's feed. But as she did so, she heard a tiny squeaking sound coming from somewhere in the feed room. She stopped what she was doing and listened, trying to locate the source. It was a tiny sound, almost like a small animal crying.

She followed the squeak and finally located the culprit in a corner, behind some feed bags. It was a tiny baby mouse! She quietly sneaked back to General's feed can and grabbed the coffee can she used to measure his grain. She crept back to the corner. The animal had moved a little, but she followed the squeaking and soon spotted him again. She quickly set the can over him. "Gotcha!"

"Got who?" David's deep voice came from the doorway. He had returned and was leaning against the jamb.

Cassy turned and triumphantly beamed at him. "I caught a mouse."

"I thought General caught it in his water bucket." He wasn't smiling but his eyes were teasing.

"Not that one. That was probably the mother. I caught a baby." She pointed to the can, which was now emitting tiny terrified squeaks.

"I see." He didn't move, just stood there looking at her excited expression. "What do you plan to do with it now?"

Cassy turned back to the can. The frightened noises were breaking her heart. "Let it go," she admitted sheepishly.

"Somehow I thought so," David said dryly. "I'll help you." He reached for the dustpan from a hook on the wall. When Cassy stood aside, he slipped it under the can and held it there while he righted the can with the baby inside. "It *is* kind of cute," he admitted, removing the dustpan and looking down in the can. "Too bad they grow up to be such destructive rodents."

Together they walked outside the barn and across the dark pasture to stop at the edge of the woods. David hunkered down and gently dumped the little mouse on a pile of leaves. They watched as it scampered away to disappear in the dark.

Cassy turned to find David's moonlit face looking at her tenderly. His arms came around her, and she allowed him to draw her to him. She tilted her head up to accept his kiss.

Once again she found her body growing warm even though it was a cool night. His kiss was tender and passionate at the same time, and Cassy found herself responding in spite of all her doubts.

He drew away first, but continued to hold her hands. "I've missed you," he said, his eyes locking with hers. She looked beautiful in the moonlight. This woman was getting to him. Did she know how much he wanted her?

Cassy knew what would happen if they stayed out in the moonlight—she was getting in over her head. "I have to go feed General." She turned abruptly and started to walk toward the barn.

"Wait!" David took two steps to catch up when she paused. "Can you come out to Pine Haven after work tomorrow?" he asked.

Cassy shook her head. "I'm going to my parents' house. We're having a late turkey dinner." She tried to read David's expression. Was he disappointed?

He lifted one eyebrow. "You're not avoiding me, are you?"

"Of course not! In fact, I was going to invite you to come with me, but you already had plans with Maggie." She looked at the ground, not wanting him to see the uncertainty in her eyes.

"Okay, then how about letting me take you to dinner after I finish here on Friday?" he suggested.

Her heart leaped with joy. "Great. I'll be here after work again, though the way things are going, it may be late."

"That's okay; I'll wait." His expression said she was worth waiting for.

She smiled happily. "It's a date. Now I'd really better feed that horse of mine before he breaks down the barn." She started to turn away again, but David grabbed her hand. Instead of letting her go, he pulled her close again and kissed her one more time.

"Okay, now you can go," he said, his voice gentle as he released her. He picked up the coffee can that had held the baby mouse and handed it to her. Wordlessly, she took it and walked back to the barn, while he went directly to his car.

On the way home, David couldn't stop thinking about her. It had been hard as anything to stay professional when she was in his class, when he had to keep watching her and touching her and act as though she didn't affect him.

Then he'd seen her in her professional uniform and realized there was a lot more to her than surface attractiveness. She was a lot older than he'd thought, and had an important job—one she did well, from what he'd seen. As he'd gotten to know her, he'd come to really like her as a person. She was a very caring lady. She was really concerned about her patients, and kids in general. She'd make a great mom someday.

Sadly his thoughts turned back to Rhonda. It was too bad they hadn't discussed having kids before they got married. At the time they were both so involved with their careers they hadn't even considered having a family. When she got pregnant, he was happy, but she wasn't. They'd quarreled bitterly. She'd refused to give up riding, insisting that her doctor said it was okay to continue as long as she felt comfortable.

Then she'd had a miscarriage. He'd tried to be supportive. But they'd quarreled again the day of his last competition, and he'd allowed his concentration to waver just enough to be dangerous. And he'd paid dearly. He'd lost his horse, the use of his legs, and his marriage. Now he'd regained his legs through hard work. He could get another horse. Did he want another wife?

Cassy was the first woman he'd been interested in in that way for a long time. He'd have to take it slow with her, make sure he didn't scare her off. She was special— no doubt about that. He'd known that the day he met her.

Now she wasn't his student anymore. They were both adults and unattached. He could tell every time he kissed her that she wanted him too. Yet she was holding back. Was she afraid of commitment? Maybe she was afraid of being hurt.

If she fell in love with him and then he left town, where would that leave her? She was the kind of woman who wanted marriage. He wasn't sure he was ready for that kind of commitment again. If he married again, he wanted it to be forever. He had to make sure he chose the right woman next time.

Suddenly he laughed at himself. *One date, and already I'm thinking about marriage! Didn't I learn anything from past experience?* He shook his head in self-rebuke.

No, he'd have to take it slow with Cassy Collins.

Chapter Seven

Thanksgiving Day was quiet at the hospital, since all but the really sick patients had been sent home. Cassy liked it that way, since it meant she had more time to devote to bedside patient care. Most of the children had family members there, so Cassy spent the majority of her time with the few who didn't. Her shift passed quickly, and then she drove home to change and pick up the pumpkin and pecan pies she'd baked the night before and begin the long drive to her parents' house. She'd already arranged for the Dobranskis to take care of General.

Her sisters and their families were already there. They all greeted her warmly and then resumed last-minute meal preparations. Cassy immediately began to help, and within minutes they had the meal on the table.

Cassy enjoyed all the noise and confusion. It was a nice change from eating alone in her apartment. Her father and sisters were all curious to know about the new man in her life, especially when she blushed as soon as they mentioned him. But she successfully dodged their questions, giving them little information other than his name and that he had been her riding instructor. After a few unsuccessful attempts at finding out more details, they gave up and moved on to other subjects.

Later, after helping clear the table and do the dishes, Cassy and her mother went back to the dining room to put away the china, leaving her sisters to finish in the kitchen.

"You haven't said much about the new man in your life," Mrs. Collins said as soon as they were alone. "But I can tell from the way your face lights up every time someone mentions him that he's special." She opened the hutch and started to place a stack of dishes inside it.

Cassy leaned back against the table, considering her answer. "Yeah, he *is* special, Mom. I really like him a lot."

"Then what's the problem?" Her mother turned and lifted her large brown eyes to meet Cassy's identical ones.

"He's the kind of guy I could fall in love with." Cassy handed her mother a stack of salad plates, smiling sheepishly.

"That's a problem?" Mrs. Collins frowned and took the plates, turning away momentarily to put them in the cabinet.

"Only because I'm not sure he wants a serious relationship, and I do."

"I see." The older woman pursed her lips as she placed the last dish in the cabinet and turned back to Cassy. "Is he seeing anyone else?"

"I don't know. That's part of the problem. He lives

at the stable run by his friend's widow. She's young and pretty, and, well. . . . '' She shrugged.

"Did the friend die recently?"

"Very. And David says that he's spending the holiday with Maggie because it'll be hard on her."

"It sounds to me like your David is a very thoughtful person. Remember when Janet's husband died?"

Cassy nodded. Her sister's husband had been killed in an accident at his construction company several years earlier.

"The hardest time for her was holidays—especially the first year." Mrs. Collins picked up Cassy's hands and squeezed them. "Has he given you any reason to think there *is* something else going on?"

Cassy shook her head. "No, and he asked me to have dinner with him tomorrow."

"Well, there you go. He must be interested in you! You go, and have a good time. And quit worrying so much!"

"Okay, I will." Cassy smiled and hugged the other woman affectionately. "Thanks, Mom. I needed a pep talk."

By the time Cassy and her mother returned to the kitchen, the other two women had finished the cleanup and were preparing to leave. Cassy hugged and kissed everyone good-bye and began the long drive home. She had to be at work again at seven, so she wearily crawled into bed as soon as she got home.

The next day Cassy went to work, anticipating another quiet day like Thanksgiving. Due to the expected low patient census, fewer staff were scheduled. But the flu virus had been rapidly spreading and several new children were admitted. Cassy was kept busy through her entire shift.

An hour before quitting time, she sank onto her chair in the nurses' station with a sigh. "This is the first time I've sat down all day," she said to Betty, the ward clerk.

"Don't look now, but Mrs. Evans is headed this way," the redhead answered. "Care to place a wager on which of us gets to work an extra shift?"

Cassy groaned. "Oh, no—I had a date tonight too." She looked up from the chart she was holding and rose as her floor supervisor entered the station. "Maybe she just wants a report," she whispered hopefully.

Betty threw her a doubtful look. "Sure," she muttered.

Cassy forced a bright smile to her lips, but the look on the gray-haired woman's face wasn't encouraging. She lowered her overweight body onto the nearest chair and turned pleading brown eyes to Cassy.

"Please tell me you can work tonight," she implored, getting right to the point. "Half my nurses have called in sick, and with the long holiday weekend, I can't reach anybody to call in."

"I do have plans . . . " Cassy started to refuse. But she gave in, seeing the worried look on the older woman's face. "But I guess I can change them."

"Thank you. I knew I could count on you. I'll be staying too, so you call me when you need a break." Mrs. Evans heaved herself off the chair and made her exit before Cassy could change her mind.

"You should have told her you couldn't do it," Betty said, swiveling her chair around to turn disapproving eyes to Cassy. "They think we're not allowed to have lives outside this hospital."

"I couldn't." Cassy sighed. "We really are short-staffed, and I felt sorry for her. Besides, I'd rather be on the good side of my boss. And I can always use the overtime pay.''

''Yeah, I guess you have a point.'' Betty noticed the phone light blinking and turned back toward it. ''But I'm glad it's you instead of me.'' She picked up the phone and said, ''Pediatrics, Ms. Duncan.''

Cassy sighed wearily. The last thing she wanted to do tonight was work an extra shift. She usually enjoyed her job, but lately the stress had been leaving her totally exhausted at the end of the day. It usually took hours to forget all the problems at the hospital and relax enough to get to sleep at night. Going out to the stable was the only thing that helped. And tonight she couldn't even do that. If only she could make a living riding and taking care of horses! But right now she needed the hospital paycheck just to keep ahead of expenses for herself and General. Any overtime she could make could be put aside for the future.

She picked up the chart she'd been working on and resumed writing. When she'd finished the last one, she called Greenwood and explained to Mr. D. that she wouldn't be out to take care of General. David was in the middle of a class, but she left a message for him, hoping he would understand, and be half as disappointed as she was.

David went directly to the Dobranskis' house to shower and change after his last lesson. He emerged from their bathroom wearing a blue polo shirt and black dress pants, his hair freshly washed and combed.

Mrs. Dobranski met him in the hall. ''I'm sorry, David, but Cassy called and told Don she has to work a double shift. She won't be able to go out tonight.''

"You mean I'm being stood up?" David asked, frowning.

"I guess so. You were in class when she called, and Don said he'd give you the message when you got done. He didn't realize you were coming to the house first."

"Can I call her back? Maybe we can meet when she gets off."

"No, they frown on personal calls at the hospital. They won't even put you through unless you tell them it's an emergency. Maybe she'll call back later. In the meantime you're welcome to stay and have dinner with us. We won't be eating for a while yet, though, not till all the horses are fed."

"Thanks. But I was looking forward to going out."

"It's a shame you got all dressed up . . . you look really nice. Poor Cassy doesn't know what she's missing."

David looked at her thoughtfully for a minute. "What time are visiting hours at the hospital?"

"Seven to nine, I think. Why?"

"I want to see Cassy tonight, even if just for a few minutes, and I think I just figured out how." He started to shrug on his jacket as he headed for the door. "Wish me luck," he added as he turned and flashed her a grin.

Mrs. Dobranski crossed her fingers and raised her hand in a farewell gesture. "I'll be rooting for you," she promised.

Once in his car, David told himself he was probably crazy to be going all the way to the hospital just on the chance he'd get to see Cassy for a few minutes. What if she wasn't really working? Maybe she'd just changed her mind about going out with him.

No, Cassy wasn't the kind of woman who would lie about that. She'd be there.

He wondered why he didn't just make other plans. Surely he could find a last-minute date. Maggie would certainly jump at the chance to go out—and he owed her a night out after all the meals she'd fed him.

But he had been looking forward to seeing Cassy tonight. In fact, after that kiss Wednesday night he'd found it hard to keep her out of his mind. Thoughts of her were interfering with his concentration. Maybe when he got to know her a little better, he'd find he didn't like her at all. Maybe it would help to get her out of his system. *Or maybe you'll fall in love with her*, said a voice inside him.

He reached the hospital and parked in the visitors' lot. No one tried to stop him as he walked through the lobby.

David took a deep breath to fortify himself. He'd forgotten how much he hated hospitals. All the mediciney smells were a brutal reminder of the two worst times of his life.

First he'd had to deal with the loss of his baby, and sit at the bedside of the woman who didn't seem to care.

Then, just weeks later, he was a patient himself. He had to deal with not only the physical pain, but the loss of his horse, and the loneliness of being left to recover in traction while his wife was continuing the career he'd lost.

This was not a place he wanted to be. But it was the only way to see Cassy tonight. He squared his shoulders, and went up to the desk. A pretty candy striper willingly gave him directions to pediatrics.

Within a few minutes, he was stepping off the elevator on Cassy's floor.

A quick glance at the nurses' station revealed another nurse and an aide, but no Cassy. David turned down a hall and started walking purposefully, glancing casually into each room as he passed.

He hadn't seen her by the time he reached the end of the hall, and he was starting to get concerned that maybe Cassy wasn't there after all. But he checked the ward at the end of the hall and started back toward the nurses' station, heading up the other side.

As he started to pass the third room, David froze in position. There were two beds and two cribs in the room, all occupied. The young girls in the beds appeared to be asleep. There was a baby in one of the cribs, also asleep. But David's eyes were held by the young woman in pastel holding an infant next to the last crib.

It was Cassy, wearing a pink smock over her white uniform, and a nurse's cap perched on her head. She was facing the doorway, but didn't notice David as she was cuddling the baby and crooning softly to it.

David folded his arms and leaned against the doorjamb to relax, in no hurry to interrupt the pleasant scene before him.

He watched contentedly as she comforted the baby and then gently laid it down in the crib. She picked up the chart at the end of the bed and started to write something as she headed toward the door, still unaware of his presence.

Suddenly, a few feet away from him, she looked up and met his eyes. Her face registered surprise, and then pleasure as she smiled happily.

''David! What are you doing here?''

He remained where he was. "I don't like being stood up." With an effort he kept from smiling, but Cassy wasn't fooled.

She closed the chart and hugged it to her. "Well, as you can see, I had a good excuse." She inclined her head toward her patients in the room.

"I think I'm jealous," he said dryly.

"Don't be. I would much rather be out with you." She smiled again, meeting his eyes.

"Any chance you can get off early?" He straightened and stepped into the hallway, allowing her to exit the room.

"I'm afraid not . . . but I haven't had my dinner break yet, if you don't mind eating in the cafeteria."

He grimaced. "Okay, I guess I'm in the right place if I get sick."

Cassy laughed. "I'll meet you there as soon as I can get someone to relieve me." She told him how to get there and went back to the nurses' station to call Mrs. Evans.

David found the cafeteria with no problem. As soon as he entered, he was greeted by nostalgic high school and college cafeteria smells of grease and overcooked food. He wrinkled his nose. *You would think a hospital would have a more healthy selection of food*, he thought, glancing over the menu of unappetizing choices as he bought himself coffee.

He took his cup and settled at a small table where he had a good view of the doorway. *Guess I should have gotten a spoon*, he thought grimly, as he took a tentative sip of the strong black brew.

He looked around the cafeteria, noticing that he was the only person alone at a table. There were a few small groups of three or four men and women in white uniforms or lab coats. The room was large, as though it were normally used for much larger crowds than tonight.

David glanced back at the doorway and saw Cassy coming in. She was talking and smiling at a man in a lab coat, and David felt an unexplained irritation. But when her gaze landed on him and locked there, he forgot everything but how good she looked. She'd removed the pink smock and was now all in white.

He got up and went to meet her. The man in the lab coat moved on, but Cassy waited till David reached her.

"Hi, are you hungry?" she asked as they headed for the food line.

"I'm not sure. . . . " he said, taking another doubtful look at the selection. "What's safe?"

"I usually stick with something vegetarian," Cassy said, reaching for a large salad and placing it on her tray. Next she chose a helping of macaroni and cheese, and finally a slice of chocolate cake.

David decided to trust her judgment and took the same. He held their glasses under the iced tea dispenser and then paid for their meals while Cassy got napkins and straws.

"At least you can't complain about the price," Cassy quipped, noting the low total for the meal.

"That's true; this is going to be a cheap date," he admitted. They settled in seats at David's original table.

"I'm afraid I don't have very long," Cassy said, unfolding her paper napkin and placing it on her lap. "But I'm glad you came. This was a nice surprise."

"Me too," David answered, smiling. He took a tentative sip of his tea, hoping it was better than the coffee. Not much.

A handsome man with black hair and dark eyes was approaching their table. He was wearing the uniform green of a surgeon. As he came up behind Cassy, he nodded at David, but placed an arm around her shoulder and leaned over the table to meet her at eye level.

"How is our little pneumonia patient tonight?" he asked in a heavy Spanish accent.

"Still spiking a temp," Cassy answered, turning her head to meet his eyes.

The man nodded thoughtfully. "I'll change the antibiotic. Everything else okay?" His glance flicked back to David, who was eyeing him suspiciously.

"Fine. Will you be up to change the order?" Cassy didn't offer to introduce them.

"Yes, as soon as I have some coffee." He smiled at her and straightened before heading to the drink line.

Cassy looked at David and found him watching her. Could that be jealousy in his eyes?

"That was Dr. Diaz," she explained. "He's the resident on duty tonight." She picked up her fork and took a bite of salad.

David didn't reply. He watched the physician warily as he bought some coffee and then went to join a table of young nurses. At least Cassy hadn't asked him to join them.

He reached for his fork. Cassy appeared to be relishing her salad—either that or she was awfully hungry. Maybe she was used to the food here. Somehow he'd lost his appetite.

Cassy ate quickly, knowing her time was limited. She was aware of the change in David's mood since the appearance of Dr. Diaz. It was kind of nice to have him jealous of her association with the handsome doctor. She considered explaining that Dr. Diaz was also a happily married man and her involvement with him was strictly as a co-worker. But she decided it wasn't necessary. The man had merely asked her a professional question, not out on a date. If David had a problem with that, he'd have to get over it.

She changed the subject instead. "How are things at Greenwood?"

David stopped chewing the bite of rubbery macaroni and forced it down. "Fine. I miss you, though. My beginners' class isn't nearly as exciting since you left."

Cassy smiled. "I miss it too. But I've been practicing what you taught me."

Just then Cassy's name was paged. She groaned. "I have to go. One of my patients must be in trouble. Will you call me?"

"How about if I take you out for a *real* dinner tomorrow?"

"Great." She took a last swallow of tea and grabbed her plate of cake as she rose. "I'll try to finish this later. Thanks for coming."

David nodded, and when she smiled into his eyes, he knew it was worth it. He watched her as she walked away and knew he'd be looking forward to the next night's dinner.

After a few more bites, he gave up on the macaroni and decided to try the cake. Not too bad—at least dessert was palatable. He was finishing the last bite when Dr. Diaz started to pass his table on his way out.

The physician noticed David watching him and changed direction to join him. He extended his hand as he reached David's table. "Hello, I'm Hector Diaz."

David rose and shook the other man's hand firmly. "David Carlyle."

"You are a friend of our Cassy, no?"

"Yes." David eyed him suspiciously, inwardly bristling at the man's possessive use of her name. He remained standing and started to gather the plates from dinner.

"You are a lucky man," the doctor continued, seemingly unaware of David's antagonistic attitude. "Our Cassy is very popular. She's a good nurse too. We would hate to lose her."

David remained silent, unsure of where this conversation was headed. He stacked the last of the plates from dinner on his tray and turned toward the door. The doctor fell into step with him.

"Are you going back up to Peds?" Dr. Diaz asked.

"Peds? Oh . . . Pediatrics. No, I don't work here. I'm leaving."

"I will give Cassy your love then, no?"

"Okay, thanks." The doctor turned toward the elevator and David headed back toward the lobby and the front door, frowning. What was that all about? Had the doc been trying to make him jealous, or was he just being friendly?

David reached the door and went out into the night more confused than ever. Whether it had been Dr. Diaz's intent or not, he'd found himself resenting the physician and his contact with Cassy, professional or not.

But he reminded himself that he had to accept the fact that she had a life completely apart from his, and if he wanted to have a relationship with her, they'd have to start spending more time together.

*   *   *

The next day at work was much the same. Cassy was kept busy and before she knew it, the day was over and it was time to head to Greenwood.

Once again, David was in the arena giving a lesson when she arrived. She changed into her jeans and finished her barn chores, then walked out to the arena to watch the rest of David's clinic.

She was the only one in the bleachers today so she knew he must know she was there. But he gave no sign of acknowledgement as his concentration was fully on the children in his class. Cassy found herself envying them as he gave individual instructions, repositioning arms and legs that had slipped out of the correct alignment. He'd make a wonderful father; he was so patient with the kids.

When David dismissed the last little girl, Cassy rose and stepped down to meet him as he came out of the arena. Although his eyes were warm, his smile seemed forced. There were unusually dark circles under his eyes and fatigue lines on his forehead.

"Hi, are we still on for dinner?" He even sounded tired.

Cassy hesitated. "Are you sure you're up to it? It looks like you've had a hard day."

"No worse than usual. It'll be fun to get out. But I'll need to shower and change first." He cast an appraising eye from Cassy's dirt-smudged face down through her T-shirt and jeans to her well-worn sneakers. "Looks like you do too. Why don't I pick you up at your apartment in about an hour?"

"Okay. What should I wear?"

"How about a dress? I bet you'd look great in a dress—I've only seen you in riding clothes or your uniform."

Cassy laughed. "Okay. See you there." She turned quickly and headed toward her car, unaware that he was still watching her appreciatively.

Back at home it didn't take long to decide what to wear, since she didn't own many dresses. She chose her favorite dark blue one with a slightly low V-neck and flattering lines. Since she'd bought it for a wedding, she had heels and a small purse to match. She arranged her hair to lie in soft waves on her shoulders and took extra care with her makeup. As a finishing touch, she put on a pair of dangling silver earrings in the shape of a horse's snaffle bit that her parents had given her last Christmas.

She was giving herself a final inspection when the doorbell rang. She opened it to find David standing there in a navy-blue suit, looking so handsome she had to stifle a gasp of pleasure.

His eyes too had darkened in pleasure at the sight of her, echoing his words when he spoke. "You look great! Maybe we should just stay here. . . . "

"Oh, no, you promised me dinner—and I'm starving." Cassy avoided the seductive look in his eyes and reached into the closet for her coat.

"Uh-oh, a hungry woman," he said wryly. "Guess I'd better get you fed."

Cassy ignored the remark and preceded him out the door. Once in the car they decided on an Italian restaurant David knew where they wouldn't need reservations. Cassy found that as long as she didn't look into his eyes he was easy to talk to.

The restaurant was small and almost filled, but the hostess was welcoming. "Hello, David," she said, her warm gaze taking in both of them. She immediately ushered them to a quiet corner. Cassy slid into the booth and David took the seat across from her. She perused the menu while he ordered wine.

"It appears that you've been here before," she remarked, peeking over the top of the menu at him. She'd noticed that the handsome Italian waiter also greeted David by name. "What would you recommend?"

He picked up his own menu and looked it over quickly. "I haven't had a bad meal here yet," he said, "but the fettucine is the best anywhere."

The waiter returned with a bottle of red wine and David sat back while he poured them each a glass and set the bottle on the table before taking their order.

"Two fettucine?" David asked, looking at Cassy for confirmation. She nodded and handed her menu back to the waiter. He took their salad orders as well, collected David's menu, and left the table.

David picked up his wineglass and lifted it in a toast. "To a new and lasting relationship."

Cassy lifted her glass to return the toast. "To a stable relationship," she said, smiling at her pun. Her eyes locked with his and stayed there, neither wanting to look away.

"Some garlic bread?" The waiter was back. Cassy and David both reluctantly pulled away to make room on the table. The aroma of the fresh-baked bread was delicious. The waiter placed the basket in the middle of their table and then deftly set a bowl of minestrone soup in front of each of them. "Can I get you anything else?" he asked, looking from one to the other.

"No, thank you," David answered, his eyes never leaving Cassy's face.

"This smells wonderful," Cassy said, reaching for

a piece of garlic bread. She purposely avoided his eyes and dipped the bread in her soup before taking a bite.

"It always is," he said, still watching her. Did she realize how beautiful she was? He watched entranced as she swallowed and then dipped again.

"You're going to have garlic breath," he teased.

"Will that be a problem?" she asked playfully.

"Not if I have some too." He reached for a piece as well, enjoying the pink flush entering her cheeks.

They ate the rest of their soup in silence. When the waiter had removed the bowls and replaced them with their salads, Cassy decided to steer the subject to a safer topic.

She picked up her salad fork and speared a piece of cucumber. "Have you always liked horses?" she asked before putting it in her mouth.

David looked thoughtful for a minute. "Ever since I saw my first cowboy movie, probably at five or six. My parents got tired of me bugging them to buy me a pony, so they took me to Greenwood for a lesson— thinking once I found out it wasn't as easy as John Wayne made it look that I'd lose interest. But they were surprised to find that once I got in the saddle, I was hooked for life!" He took his own bite of salad and chewed before continuing.

"So I started taking lessons, and Mr. D. let me clean stalls to pay for them. Back then I was mainly interested in speed—all the cowboy stuff like barrel racing and cutting cows. It's a wonder Mr. D. put up with me— and that I didn't kill myself." He shook his head and took another bite.

"So how'd you go from Western games to riding English?" Cassy asked, fascinated.

David smiled. "Well, I used to think English was

for sissies. But when a bunch of us from the stable took a field trip to the American Invitational in Tampa one year, I was totally impressed. We got to walk out on the course before it started and stand next to those huge jumps, which are about six feet high, and some six feet wide. I couldn't imagine the thrill of riding a horse over something that big. Later, when I saw people doing it—and making it look so easy—I knew I had to try it.''

"How old were you then?"

"Early teens, I guess. It was right before my dad got transferred and we had to move to Texas. We found a good teacher for me there, and I took English lessons and learned to jump. I discovered that liking horses was a great way to meet girls so I never lost interest. My parents insisted that I go to college, so I got a degree in agriculture. But all I really wanted to do was Grand Prix. I did well at local shows, riding other people's horses till I got out of college and then bought Jet and rode for myself. We were doing pretty well until the accident. And I guess you know what happened after that.'' His face darkened, and he concentrated on his salad.

Not sure if he was remembering the end of his marriage or the death of his horse, Cassy decided to pursue another topic. While she tried to think of one, the waiter returned with their main course.

"And how about you?" David asked as soon as the waiter withdrew. "When did you get interested in horses?"

"Like you—as a kid from old *Bonanza* reruns. I was in love with Little Joe—and his horse. Then when I discovered the *Black Stallion* books, I was really hooked. But we didn't have any horses nearby or a place to ride. I didn't get much chance until I moved to Orlando to take the job at Community Hospital.''

''My parents always encouraged my sisters and me to do noncompetitive sports, like dance classes. They didn't want us to have to compete against each other as my mom and aunt had had to do. My mom was scared of horses anyway, so she especially discouraged me. But it's always been a dream of mine.''

''So how did you finally get started?'' David continued to listen intently as Cassy told him the story of how she'd met the Dobranskis and they'd taken her under their wing.

''So you've only been riding a little over a year?'' he asked, sitting back to finish his wine when she paused to take another bite of fettucine.

She nodded, her mouth still full.

''Have you ever thought about showing?''

She swallowed. ''Well, yes, but I don't think I'm good enough. . . . ''

He leaned toward her, his expression sincere. ''I've seen you ride, remember?'' She looked up and caught him looking intensely into her eyes.

''You are definitely good enough for local shows.'' His mouth turned up slightly. ''You've had the best teacher there is, right?''

She smiled at his lack of modesty. ''That's true.''

''Okay, so that excuse won't work anymore. I want you to enter the next Greenwood show.''

''Are you sure I'm ready?''

''Absolutely. I'll even coach you. And we can borrow whatever show equipment you don't have.''

''That's almost everything,'' she said ruefully. ''And won't your other students be jealous if you help me?''

"Maybe. But free coaching of a friend is not the same as being paid to teach. Besides, I won't be judging. Now, no more excuses!" He went back to concentrating on his meal.

But Cassy was losing her appetite. The idea of showing was exciting and terrifying at the same time. Did she really want to do it? She continued to toy with the rest of her meal for a few more minutes and then finally laid down her fork and sipped at her wine.

"What's wrong?" David asked. "Surely this meal is better than that cafeteria food you're used to."

Cassy smiled. "Oh, yes. I'm just kind of nervous at the idea of showing."

David nodded. "I understand. The first time is scary. Each time after that gets a little easier. But the adrenaline high you get before a show is so exciting, you may get hooked and decide that's all you want to do."

"Is that what happened to you?"

"At first. And I enjoyed it for a long time. But I was starting to get tired of it—even before I got hurt." His expression turned grim. "I haven't told anybody else this, but I think I was secretly glad I had an excuse to quit."

"Why?"

"I was able to end my showing career before I reached the top instead of making it and then gradually heading back down." He smiled ruefully and paused to take a drink of wine before continuing.

"Anyway, I'm much happier with what I'm doing now. I'm still working with horses, and good people—without the stress.

"Speaking of stress," he added, looking pointedly at Cassy, "don't you get tired of all those long hours at the hospital?"

Cassy set down her wineglass and grimaced. "Yes. On slow days I enjoy my work because I have time to spend with my patients. But days like yesterday, when we are short-staffed, it seems like all I do is paperwork, and I'm running in and out of rooms so fast I barely know the patient's name. It's so frustrating!"

"Do you ever think about giving it up?"

Cassy frowned in surprise. "Give up nursing?"

He nodded. "Yes, or at least cut down your hours?"

She shook her head. "Not really. What would I do? I need the money to support my 'habit.' "

At David's surprised arch of one eyebrow, she laughed. "My horse."

He chuckled. "But maybe you could work part-time as a nurse and do something at the stable the rest of the time to earn General's keep. You're good with kids, and I bet you'd make a good instructor. Maybe you could teach beginning lessons."

Cassy's eyes widened. "Do you really think so?"

"Absolutely. It's an option worth considering. And I'd sure like to get to see more of you."

Cassy met his eyes and her heart skipped a beat at the sincerity she saw flickering in the depths of his gaze. After declining the waiter's offer of coffee or dessert, David paid the bill and escorted her outside. Back inside his car he asked, "Would you like to go someplace else?"

Cassy shook her head. "No, thanks. I think we're both tired after a busy week."

David started up the car, and they drove back to her building, making small talk along the way. When he parked near her apartment, Cassy invited him in for coffee.

Her heart was pounding as she entered the kitchen

to begin making the coffee, unsure of what would develop. How far did she want it to go? She opened the cabinet and reached for the instant coffee when David's arms came around her from behind and circled her waist. The coffee forgotten, she turned and was enveloped in his strong embrace. Her head tipped back of its own accord and her lips parted to meet his. He kissed her. Instantly she lost all sense of reality as a delicious warmth crept over her body.

Suddenly the shrill ring of the phone next to them caused her to jerk away and look at it in alarm.

"Let it ring," David growled, nuzzling her neck.

Cassy hesitated, not wanting the joy of being in his arms to end. "I better get it," she said on the third ring. "No one would call me this late unless it was important."

"Hello?" It was an effort not to giggle as David continued to plant tiny kisses on her neck.

"Cassy? It's Maggie. Is David there?" Her heart sank. Another emergency. She handed the phone to David. "For you."

He frowned in puzzlement, but took the phone. "Hello?"

Cassy stepped out of his other arm and started to reach for the coffee again. She couldn't help but overhear David's side of the conversation.

"Maggie! What's wrong?" His expression was concerned but quickly changed to anger. "Rhonda! What does she want? Okay, if she calls again, tell her I'll be home in half an hour. I'll call her from there." He slammed down the phone and stared at it for a moment before turning to Cassy.

"I'm sorry," he said, his voice calm but his eyes smoldering. "My ex-wife has been calling Maggie, trying to reach me all night. She wouldn't tell Maggie what it's about, but she said it's important."

"Would you like to call from here?" Cassy asked, continuing to fill her teapot with water.

"Well. . . . " He hesitated. "No, I'd better do it from home 'cause she may need some information I have there. Thanks anyway." He slipped his arms around her waist again, and she turned to meet his kiss. Somehow the mood wasn't the same.

"I'll probably see you tomorrow," he said, pulling away. He walked back to the living room. She followed him to the door and picked up his coat, which he'd thrown on the couch when he came in. Cassy could tell by the distracted way he reached for it that his mind was on what Rhonda was up to. He gave her another quick kiss before going out the door.

Cassy locked it behind him, feeling a mixture of disappointment and relief. Once again they'd been interrupted just when they were beginning to really know each other. She definitely felt rejected. He left her arms to call his ex-wife just because she wanted him to?

She bit her lip as a chilling thought occurred to her. Maybe he wasn't over Rhonda. He loved her enough to marry her once. Just because she hurt him didn't mean he didn't still care.

Cassy went back in her kitchen and put the coffee things away. The last thing she needed was caffeine to keep her awake all night. She'd have enough trouble sleeping as it was, wondering if her relationship with David had a chance.

Chapter Eight

By the next night, Cassy had even more reason to doubt that she and David could build a relationship. When she arrived at Greenwood, she discovered that David had canceled all his lessons for the day.

"Why?" she asked Mrs. Dobranski, as she gathered her equipment from the tack room. "Is something wrong?"

"I hope not," Mrs. D. said grimly, handing her General's tack box. "Maggie sounded kind of worried when she called to tell us this morning. Apparently he dropped everything to hop on a plane early this morning to go see Rhonda. All he would tell Maggie was that he might have a surprise when he got back. I do hope they're not going to reconcile."

"Is that what Maggie thinks?" Cassy tried to appear casual but her heart felt knotted in her throat. She started to walk toward General's stall.

Mrs. Dobranski followed her while she answered. "I don't know. Maggie never was real fond of Rhonda, especially after the divorce. I think the feeling was mutual, so Rhonda probably wouldn't tell her anything. If she sweet-talked David into flying up to see her, she sure wouldn't tell Maggie how or why.''

"Did he say when he'd be back?''

"No, but he asked Maggie to postpone his meeting tomorrow.''

"If you hear any more, will you let me know?'' Cassy picked up her curry comb and began to furiously attack General's dusty coat.

"Sure, hon. You and David are starting to see quite a bit of each other, aren't you?'' Mrs. D. had followed her into the stall and was standing on the other side of General, rubbing his neck. Her knowing eyes took in the sudden change in her young friend's mood.

"We were.'' Cassy concentrated on a particularly matted spot on the horse's withers. "But he seems to be too busy lately.''

"Well, he *is* a busy man. But he'll make time if he wants to. I just wish I knew what Rhonda was up to. She hurt him so badly once. He doesn't deserve that.'' The older woman gave General a final pat and walked back to the stall door. "Try not to worry, Cassy. If he goes back to her now, it means he never got over her. You couldn't build a relationship over that.''

Cassy nodded ruefully and continued grooming General while Mrs. Dobranski went back to the office. *What do I do now? Do I sit around and wait to see if he goes back to Rhonda?* She continued to brush with a vengeance until General's coat was gleaming. Finally satisfied, Cassy returned her things to the tack room and sought out Mrs. Dobranski.

She found her seated at the desk in the office, apparently trying to balance the ledgers.

"Please come in." The older woman seemed glad for an excuse to take another break.

Cassy entered and sat stiffly in the seat facing the desk. "I need a new riding instructor," she said without emotion.

Mrs. Dobranski closed the ledger book and looked at Cassy with a somewhat puzzled expression. "I'm sure David will be coming back to finish his clinics. He's the best there is."

"I know. But I don't want to have him for a teacher anymore—no matter what happens."

"I see." Mrs. Dobranski chewed her pencil thoughtfully for a moment. "Well, you're too advanced now for your old class. My husband could give you private lessons—or we could recommend someone at another stable."

"I'd like to stay here, and private lessons with Mr. D. would be fine. When can I start?"

Mrs. Dobranski hesitated a moment, as though about to object, then moved the pile of papers and ledgers on the desk to reveal the large calendar underneath. "He's taking over David's classes for today, but could probably do one this evening or tomorrow."

"How's tomorrow at one o'clock?"

"Fine."

"Okay, great. Put me down." Cassy rose to go. "Guess I'll try to get some practice in." Mrs. Dobranski didn't comment as she recorded the lesson and thoughtfully watched Cassy leave.

Cassy stopped at the tack room again to pick up a saddle and bridle, then tacked up General and led him out to an empty pasture. Once in the saddle, she began to relax and forget about her confusion over her relationship with David. She concentrated on perfecting her balance and position, and forced herself to blot out everything else.

Finally, after nearly two hours in the saddle, both she and General were exhausted. She turned him out and finished her barn chores before heading back home for a hot bath. There was no message from David, but that didn't surprise her.

Later she curled up on her couch with a pile of old horse magazines. She leafed through them absently, not sure what she was looking for. Suddenly she stopped as she found what her subconscious had remembered. It was an article about David and Rhonda, with a large picture of them together.

She's gorgeous, Cassy thought, looking at the happily smiling slim beauty in riding attire. A slightly younger-looking David, also in riding attire, was standing with his arms around her, also smiling. This was her competition? Cassy's heart sank. How could she compete with his first love? Happiness was written all over their faces.

Other pictures with the article showed them separately with their horses, going over jumps. Rhonda was not only lovely, she had shared a part of David's life that Cassy could only dream about. She skimmed the article. It told how they had met at a show and fallen in love almost instantly. They'd married soon after and traveled together. Though they sometimes competed in the same shows, they were quoted as saying it didn't interfere with their marriage.

Sadly, Cassy closed the magazine and tossed it back on the pile. Why torture herself? If he wanted Rhonda, there was nothing she could do about it. She certainly wasn't going to throw herself at him. Or sit around waiting for him to call. She'd get on with her life. That decision made, she went to bed.

The next day, Cassy's lesson with Mr. D. went well. He was surprised at her progress since her last class and had mostly positive things to say.

Walking back to the barn with her after the lesson, Mr. Dobranski commented, "I agree with David that you're ready to show."

"He told you that?"

"Sure did. He also asked if I'd mind if he coached you on the side as long as he wasn't your official instructor."

"When was that?" David had just mentioned it to her Friday night.

"This morning on the phone." He stopped and smiled at Cassy's startled expression. "He didn't call you?"

Cassy halted General and turned to her teacher, frowning slightly. "No . . . of course, I was at church this morning. And I didn't put my machine on. What else did he say?"

"He'll be back in a few days, after he takes care of a few things. I'll let him tell you about it," he said mysteriously. "I need to get back to the office now. Let me know when you want to have another lesson." He turned down the path to the barn and walked ahead, leaving Cassy to follow behind, pondering this new bit of information.

David didn't call that night or the next three. Cassy threw herself into work and fit in two more private lessons in the evenings. Convinced that he must be reconciling with Rhonda, Cassy did her best to forget about David Carlyle. But the harder she tried, the more it hurt. She couldn't get the picture of him with Rhonda out of her mind.

On Thursday she was in the tiny medicine room in back of the nurses' station when Leona, one of the LPNs, came looking for her. She was in the middle of measuring out some liquid Tylenol and almost spilled it when the other nurse suddenly stuck her head in the doorway.

"There you are! There's a good-looking man at the desk asking for you!" The husky black woman's face was grinning ear to ear. "I offered to help him, but he wanted you."

Cassy frowned. "Who is he?" She finished pouring the medicine and put the bottle away.

"A Mr. Carlyle? I don't think we have a patient with that last name. But you'd better go see him before *I* try to convince him to settle for *me* instead." The LPN gave her an impish wink and left to resume her own duties.

David! What could he be doing here? Surely he wouldn't seek her out at work to tell her he was going back to Rhonda. Her heart pounding, Cassy recorded the Tylenol and picked up the small plastic medicine cup as she went back into the nurses' station.

She had no trouble finding him. He was standing at the front of the desk talking to Bonnie, the pretty young ward clerk. Cassy heard the ripple of flirtatious feminine laughter clear across the station.

But when he caught Cassy's eyes with his over the top of Bonnie's head, nothing mattered but that he was there.

"Can you get away for lunch?" he asked in that familiar deep voice.

"No, I've already had my lunch break," she said truthfully. "But let me just give this medication, and

I'll get someone to cover for a few minutes." He nodded, and she hurried into Bobby's room to give him the Tylenol. After making sure he was comfortable, she found Sue, the other RN on duty, and told her she was taking a short break.

"Would this have anything to do with that man causing such a stir in the nurses' station?" Sue asked, grinning.

Cassy blushed. "Yes, do you mind?"

The other nurse shook her head. "Not at all, but don't be long. We're getting some new admissions any time now from Emergency."

Cassy hurried back to the station to find David. The other nurses were all busy, and the ward clerk was on the phone, so he was leaning against the wall, casually watching the corridor.

As soon as he spotted her, he straightened and came forward to meet her. "All set?"

"Yes, let's go into the staff lounge—but I just have a few minutes." She led him to a doorway and preceded him inside. Luckily it was vacant. She turned to face him as he shut the door behind him.

"What's going on?"

"I missed you." He took her hands and started to draw her toward him.

"You could have called." Cassy stepped back, resisting the urge to fall into his arms.

"I did. You didn't answer. Then I decided I'd rather surprise you." He met her challenging eyes coolly.

Cassy pulled away and turned, hugging her arms as she took a deep breath. Surely he wouldn't call it a surprise if he were going back to Rhonda. "So nothing has changed?"

"What do you mean?" He sounded puzzled.

"Did you go to see Rhonda?" She still couldn't look at him.

"Yes."

He wasn't making this easy. "Why?" Unable to take the suspense any more, she turned back and looked into his eyes, now a cold steel blue.

"She had a good reason for wanting me to come." He was becoming irritated with Cassy's accusing attitude. "I was hoping you'd be happy for me." He paused, unsure why he was feeling defensive.

Just then there was a short rap on the door and Leona stuck her head in. "I'm sorry, Cassy, but both those admissions are here and Sue needs you."

"Okay." The LPN withdrew, and Cassy turned apologetically to David. "I have to go." Her eyes were questioning. Was this the "let's be friends" speech?

"Can you come out to Pine Haven after work?" David knew this wasn't the time to explain.

"I guess so. Why?" Cassy took a step toward the door, and reached for the handle.

"I'll show you when you get there—Wait." He took a step too, and pushed the door shut again as he leaned toward her and kissed her lips. Before she could resist, he drew away and opened the door. "See you later."

She stepped out and headed toward the nurses' station. He followed, but turned toward the elevator. Cassy looked back once and caught him turning to glance back. Their eyes met, and he smiled. Surely he wasn't going to break up with her after that?

The rest of the afternoon was busy, and Cassy didn't have time to consider anything but getting her job done.

After signing off the last chart and giving her report to the evening shift, she gladly punched out and headed for her car.

On the way to Pine Haven, she debated whether or not to go. What could the surprise be? He said he wanted her to be happy for him. What if he and Rhonda were going to remarry?

Maybe he'd even brought her with him! No, she couldn't believe that. He wouldn't have come to see her at the hospital, and he certainly wouldn't have kissed her, if he planned to reunite with his ex-wife. But what could she have wanted that was so important he had to fly up to see her right away?

Cassy's thoughts went back and forth all the way to Pine Haven. *If nothing else, he's got me curious,* she thought. She finally pulled in the drive. David's car was parked by Maggie's house, so she pulled in beside it.

Everything looked much the same as the last time she was there for her lesson with David. Then she noticed a horse trailer hooked up to a large truck with Texas tags parked under some trees. That hadn't been there before.

"Hi, Cassy, come see David's surprise!" Maggie, dressed in tight jeans and a sweatshirt, was calling to her from the side of the house.

Cassy hurried around the house and saw that Maggie and a few other people were watching a horse and rider in the riding ring. As she got closer, she could tell it was David on a beautiful black stallion.

"Isn't he gorgeous?" Maggie asked excitedly. The pretty brunette motioned toward the arena and climbed up on the fence to watch.

Cassy nodded affirmatively. She had to agree, no matter which of the two in the ring Maggie was referring to. She joined Maggie and leaned on the rail, watching in awe as horse and rider moved as one, galloping around the small ring. When he noticed

Cassy, David slowed to a trot and brought the stallion over to stand in front of her.

"What do you think?" he asked, locking eyes with her.

"He's beautiful. Is he yours?"

"Yes." He turned to Maggie. "Would you mind cooling him down for me?"

"Sure." Maggie didn't need to be asked twice. She agilely jumped down from the rail and took the horse's reins.

David dismounted and climbed the fence to join Cassy. "Come on," he said, taking her hand. "Let's go to my trailer to talk."

Cassy fell into step beside him, and they began walking. "Is he what Rhonda had to show you?"

"Yes. She heard his owner was willing to sell him and knew I'd be interested. He's a full brother to Jet."

"The horse who died in the accident?"

"Yeah. I'd ridden several other horses in Grand Prix, but none of them came close to Jet in ability or heart. When he died, I was so busy feeling sorry for myself that I didn't even want to think about replacing him. Rhonda told me then I should try to buy this colt, but I wasn't interested. Besides, I couldn't even walk, much less ride. By the time I was physically ready, he'd been sold. By then my marriage was over and I was trying to forget everything that reminded me of show jumping."

"Do you think you'll go back now?"

"I don't know. I still can't ride for any length of time without pain. But I want to train Ebony for it. If he's as good as I think he is, he can do it—even if I have someone else ride him."

They had reached the trailer and he held the door open. Cassy preceded him in. The trailer was small but clean and neat. It had several windows which were open, allowing the late-afternoon sun to warm it.

"How about a cool drink?" David led the way to the kitchen and held the refrigerator door open, revealing a selection of soft drinks—and not much else.

Cassy helped herself to a root beer and leaned back against the counter. She popped the top and took a sip before speaking. "So Rhonda found out Ebony was for sale and called to tell you?"

"Yeah." David took a drink for himself and motioned for her to follow him to the living room. Once settled on the couch facing the sunset, he continued. "That was why I left so suddenly. I went directly from the airport to his stable. He was even better than Rhonda had told me. His owner needed money and accepted my first offer. Then I spent the rest of the morning making arrangements to get him here." David stretched out his legs and rested his head against the back of the couch.

"Did you haul him yourself?"

"No, I sent him off that same day. But I still had to see Rhonda and settle some things. I flew home today and arrived not long before he did."

"You must be tired."

"A little. But excited too. And really glad to have settled things." He raised his arms over his head and stretched.

"You mean with Rhonda?" Cassy sat down on the other end of the couch and tucked her outside leg behind her other ankle. She twisted to face him.

"Partly. We did a lot of talking. I think we've gotten past all the anger and bitterness and can be friends again. In fact, I may get her to ride Ebony in competition when the time comes."

"Really? You must still think a lot of her." Cassy tried not to let him know she was feeling those pangs of jealousy again.

"Well, she's one of the best riders I know—next to me, of course." He grinned slyly.

"Of course." Cassy smiled too.

"But I also decided to sell my house and dispose of everything else that was still there."

Cassy set down her drink and looked at him in amazement. "Then you're moving here for good?"

He met her eyes. "Everything I want is here now."

The intense look in his eyes frightened Cassy. Was she ready for this? She looked away toward the window and suddenly noticed the sun was almost gone.

"I still need to feed General!" She gasped, jumping to her feet.

"Don't you think the Dobranskis will take care of him?"

"They would, but I've already relied on them too much. Besides, I know you're tired." She leaned over to give him a good-bye kiss. As their lips touched, he grabbed her around the waist and pulled her onto his lap.

"I'm not *that* tired," he growled. Laughing, Cassy settled comfortably in his arms, drawing her own around him.

Just as their lips were meeting for the second time, the phone rang. Cassy giggled.

David shook his head. "I don't believe this!"

They disentangled and stood together. He picked up the phone on the third ring. "Hello? Yes, can you hold just a minute?" He put his hand over the receiver and turned back to Cassy. "It's business and may take a while. . . ."

"Okay, I'll see you tomorrow." Cassy gave him a

quick kiss and let herself out. She turned back to wave as she shut the door, but he was already reaching for his clipboard on the counter, his brows knit together in concentration as he listened to the speaker on the phone.

Cassy smiled anyway and walked to her car with a renewed bounce to her step, her spirits soaring. She was in love, really and truly, for the first time in her life. She knew that now, and she thought he felt the same.

Chapter Nine

Cassy did call David that night after getting home from Greenwood. He told her the business call had been from another stable in Orlando wanting him to do a clinic for them.

They saw each other at Greenwood or spoke on the phone every day for the next week. David was kept busy between his clinic lessons and making arrangements for the show at Grand Cypress. He spent every hour that wasn't scheduled training Ebony.

But Cassy didn't mind. She was busy enough herself between work and taking care of General. She scheduled her private riding lessons for her days off. It was getting dark so early in the evening now that she rarely got to ride after work. Although David occasionally gave her a few tips, he rarely had more than a few minutes to speak to her while she was riding.

It was early December now, and the weather had changed from brisk and invigorating to extremely cold and bone chilling. The horses seemed to enjoy it, and put on a show of running around and playfully bucking and rearing whenever they were turned out. The Dobranskis added to their nightly routine, putting blankets on all the horses and mixing salt into their food to make sure they drank enough water to compensate for less grass and more hay.

The day of the December show at Greenwood was approaching. Cassy had bought or borrowed everything she needed for herself and her horse. She spent several evenings the week before saddle-soaping and oiling her saddle and bridle. General was clipped and his coat gleamed from all the extra grooming she'd managed to fit in. Even if they didn't perform well, Cassy was satisfied that they would look good.

The morning of the show she arrived soon after dawn, and already the stable was bustling with activity. Several horse trailers were parked on the grounds, and people of all ages were busy unloading, grooming, or exercising their horses.

Cassy had attended shows there before as a spectator, and had sensed a special air of excitement on show days. Today was even more exciting because she would be entering her first competition. She had scarcely slept the night before and after waking early had decided she might as well go to the stable. Her own classes would not start until late morning, but maybe she could see if there was anything she could do to help someone else get ready.

She parked her car in the usual place in front of the barn and went inside. Mr. Dobranski was coming down the aisle, a worried expression on his face.

"What's wrong?" she asked.

"General's off his feed. He wouldn't touch his grain and is just picking at his hay. Can you try walking him out to see how he acts before I call a vet?"

Cassy's heart sank. If General was sick she couldn't show. The butterflies of excitement she'd been feeling turned to ones of fear. What if something was really wrong with him?

Mr. Dobranski went on down the hall, not waiting for an answer. Cassy stopped in the tack room long enough to grab General's halter and lead rope, and then went quickly to his stall.

The horse didn't nicker or show any interest in her approach. He was standing lethargically in his stall. This was totally unlike him, and Cassy began to get really worried. She entered the stall, and he allowed her to slip his halter on without resistance.

Cassy pushed the stall door open and led him outside. They walked slowly down the center aisle while she tried to watch him closely.

Mr. Dobranski returned as they reached the rear doors of the barn. "Trot him out," he said to Cassy.

General didn't respond to the first tug on the lead as he usually did. Cassy tried again, and the horse trotted a few steps and stopped. She looked questioningly at Mr. Dobranski.

"Wait," he said, "I think he's limping. Let me check his hooves." He disappeared into the barn for a moment, and then came out, carrying a hoof pick. "Let's see that left rear foot."

Cassy stepped to General's left side and leaned against his hip, forcing him to put his weight on his right side. Then she ran her hand down the back of his rear leg until he obediently lifted the foot. Mr. Dobranski leaned over and scraped out the dirt and manure around the underside of the hoof with the pick, then turned the instrument over and used the brush on the other end to clean out the rest.

"Yep," he said, "there's an abscess, see?" He pointed to the swollen sore on the fleshy part of the foot.

"Is that bad?" Cassy asked.

"No, it's easy to fix. At least we know that's why he didn't eat his breakfast. But you won't be able to ride him for a few days."

Cassy sighed. She was glad to know it wasn't anything serious. But it sure would change her plans for the day. She waited while Mr. Dobranski got the necessary equipment and assisted as he drained and treated the abscess. Then she made sure General was settled back in his stall before going outside to see how show preparations were coming along.

Several more horse trailers had arrived, and people and horses were scattered everywhere in between. Most of the horses were being ridden, lunged in circles on long lines, or tied to their trailers, contentedly munching hay from hay nets hanging next to them.

A few children and young adults were wandering around or riding, dressed in either full English attire with breeches, hunt coats, and hard hats, or Western style with dressy Western shirts and jeans topped with cowboy hats. But most of the people grooming and exercising horses were dressed practically, as Cassy was, in sweatshirts and jeans, for the messy jobs of getting the horses ready.

"Hi, Cassy," a friendly female voice called to her. She turned toward the voice and smiled a welcome. It was Maggie, leading her buckskin mare, Lady.

Cassy reached out and patted the horse as they came up to her. "She looks beautiful," she commented, noticing the shiny coat and perfectly groomed mane and tail on Lady.

"Thanks," Maggie said. "I hope I can keep her this

way till my Western Pleasure class this afternoon. Mr. Dobranski said I can use one of his extra stalls. Do you know where it is?''

"Yeah, he put her name on it. I'll show you." Cassy fell into step beside them.

"Are you excited about your first show?" Maggie asked as they continued toward the barn.

"Not anymore," Cassy answered sadly. "General has an abscess, so I'll have to wait till next month." She bit her lip to still the tears of disappointment threatening to surface.

"Can't you ride another horse?"

"No, I haven't ridden any others here since I bought General. I wouldn't feel comfortable on another horse."

"Why don't you ride Lady?"

Cassy looked at the other woman in surprise. Her wide blue eyes looked sincere. "Well. . . . "

"I mean it. You've ridden her before—David said you did fine. I've shown her before and done pretty well. It would be a shame to have to wait, after all your preparation."

"I don't know. I hate to take your horse. . . . "

"I'm not showing her till this afternoon, so we'll have plenty of time for a tack change. And it will be better for her to have a warm-up class." Maggie reached over and squeezed Cassy's hand. "Come on, I insist."

Cassy was beginning to get caught up in the other woman's enthusiasm. She met her eyes and saw nothing but an honest desire to help. "Okay." She smiled, starting to feel excited again.

"Great." They had reached the barn. Mr. Dobranski's voice was coming over the loudspeaker welcoming everyone to the show and announcing the first halter class. Cassy showed Maggie the stall reserved for Lady and went to check on General.

Her gelding seemed to be feeling better. He had finally eaten his sweet feed and was munching his hay. He turned his big head and looked at her with a piece of hay sticking comically out of the side of his mouth.

Cassy smiled and patted his neck. ''You just wanted some extra attention today, huh?'' Satisfied that he'd be okay, she went back to her car to get her show equipment together. The first class was already over, and the second was in the ring. She'd better get moving, since her Walk Trot Pleasure class was right after the fifth halter class.

Cassy made her way to registration. It only took a few minutes to fill out the form and pay her fee. Clutching her number card she headed back to her car.

Although David's red Miata was parked in its usual place near the front of the barn, Cassy still hadn't seen him. Several of his students were showing today, so she knew he'd be kept busy.

''Have you seen David?'' she asked Maggie when she returned to the barn carrying her newly polished saddle and bridle.

''Not since we got here,'' the brunette answered. ''He helped me load Lady and followed us in his car. As soon as I unloaded, he left to find Mr. Dobranski. Why? Do you need him?''

''No, I was just wondering how he'll feel about my riding Lady. I've been practicing on General.''

''I'm sure he won't object. He told me you're a good rider.''

Cassy felt herself growing warm with pleasure. He must really think so if he told someone else. She put the saddle down outside the stall and went in to help Maggie with the bridle.

Maggie put away the grooming brushes and took the bridle from her. "I wish I'd brought my English bridle," she said. "Lady is used to it. But this should work okay." She slipped it on expertly. General's head was larger than the mare, but by moving the buckles up a few notches, she made an acceptable fit.

Next they put on Cassy's saddle pad, newly washed and white as snow. The saddle fit the mare, though General's girth was too large. A trip to the tack room located one that would fit, and Cassy buckled it on.

Mr. Dobranski was announcing the last halter class as the two women finished tacking up Lady. Cassy quickly went back to the office and changed into her tan show breeches, tan shirt, and navy hunt coat. She attached a stock pin at her throat and pulled on her boots.

When she finished, Maggie was waiting outside the barn with Lady. "You look great," she approved. "Let me put on your number."

Cassy took the reins and turned her back to Maggie while the other woman pinned the cardboard number to her jacket. She placed her black velvet hard hat on her head and tucked stray hairs into the net protecting her ponytail.

Maggie held the mare as Cassy mounted. "Good luck," she said. "I'll be rooting for you."

"Thanks." Cassy took the reins. Her stomach was tied in knots now, as she realized it was almost time for her class. The spirited mare immediately began prancing around. Mr. Dobranski announced that the first- and second-place winners of each halter class should enter the ring for the judging of Grand and

Reserve Halter champions, and Walk Trot Pleasure should enter the warm-up ring.

Oh, no, not already, Cassy thought. Well, she didn't have much choice. She headed toward the warm-up ring. Lady was feeling frisky, and continued to prance. *I wish I had time to practice on her,* Cassy thought. *She's not used to the bridle or me, or even this place. I hope I'm not making a mistake. . . .*

She tried to take deep breaths and calm herself, as David had taught her. Lady seemed to be responding. The Grand and Reserve halter horses exited the arena just as Cassy and Lady entered the warm-up ring. They circled it once and entered the main ring. Lady was still prancing, apparently feeling pretty good. She was under control, and Cassy was starting to relax as they found a position on the rail.

But then suddenly a small, wildly yipping dog with a leash trailing it slipped under the rail right in front of Lady. The horse shied and jumped sideways, nearly unseating Cassy. The dog was under her front hooves and, still barking, started running in circles and biting at her legs. The horse seized the bit in her teeth and lunged forward, starting to gallop.

Cassy almost lost her balance when the horse suddenly changed direction. But she quickly regained it and held on as the mare started to run. She wasn't aware of anything around her as the rail and the spectators passed by in a blur. She could only concentrate on sitting back and slowing the horse.

David had been busy all morning. After seeing Lady safely unloaded, he had left Maggie to help Mr. Dobranski check the arena and ascertain that all the equipment was working properly. He'd introduced himself to the judge and made sure everything was to his liking. Since then, he'd been occupied with his students, assuring himself that they were prepared for their classes.

Mr. Dobranski told him General was lame, so Cassy wouldn't be showing. He'd looked for her in the crowd since he knew she'd be upset, but so far he hadn't seen her.

The Walk Trot Pleasure class was entering the ring, and David stood at the rail to watch. Even though Cassy wouldn't be there as planned, several of his other beginning students would be.

His eyebrows raised in surprise. Cassy was out there on Lady! Then he frowned with concern. Lady was obviously feeling her oats.

What happened next seemed almost like slow motion. David watched in horror as the tiny dog ran in front of Lady. The second he realized Cassy was in danger, he leaped the fence in one fluid motion.

Cassy and the horse were on the opposite side of the arena, but when Lady started to gallop, she was headed toward David.

The other horses and riders froze in position on the rail, giving them plenty of room on the inside.

David quickly assessed the situation as he ran. Someone grabbed the dog and got it out of the way. He reached the center of the arena and grabbed Lady's reins just as Cassy regained control and pulled her up.

"Are you okay?" David asked, gasping as he tried to catch his breath.

Cassy was breathing fast too, and was flushed from excitement. "Yes." She nodded, patting Lady to reassure her.

"Good," he said. "I'll withdraw you from the class." He dropped the reins.

"No!" Cassy was near tears now that her fear was slipping away. "I want to do it." She raised her chin and met his stern face.

"As your teacher, I want you out of here." His voice was low but angry. "You're not experienced enough to ride this horse."

"You're not my teacher anymore," she said defiantly, tossing her head. "I can do it." She picked up the reins and started walking toward the rail. As soon as she reached it, the announcer asked the riders to resume walking their horses.

David shook his head in disbelief. He'd ordered her to get out, and she'd defied him! He didn't know whether to admire her spunk or have her head examined. Right now he wanted to strangle her. He quickly slipped out of the ring and counted to ten before finding a place to watch.

Lady was still chomping at the bit, walking faster than she should. But Cassy was even more determined now, wanting to prove herself to David. She kept the horse under control.

When they had all made a circle around the arena, they were asked to trot. Lady gladly picked up the faster gait. Cassy posted, making sure she was on the correct diagonal. This wasn't so bad after all. They passed the bleachers.

"Way to go, Cassy," she heard Maggie's encouraging voice. She smiled. This was almost fun.

"Walk your horses," came the command. Lady obediently slowed to a walk. "And reverse."

Cassy and Lady turned and changed direction.

David had gone back to his original position outside the rail, where he was watching grimly. He had to hand it to Cassy—she had guts. Too bad she didn't have the sense to go with them. There was no way she'd place in this class. With ten riders and only six ribbons, no judge in his right mind would award a place to a horse that had tried to run off.

Cassy looked good, though. If they were judging on how good the rider looked, she'd have a chance. He watched as she trotted by, not seeing him, a slight smile on her face. She seemed to have regained control. Maybe she was right to stay in there after all.

The horses were asked to line up before the judge. Cassy took a place near the end of the row. The judge walked down the row and asked each rider to back. Lady balked a little, but did it on the third try. David chewed his lip nervously. This class seemed to be taking forever. He wanted Cassy out of there and off that horse.

The runner took the results note from the judge and passed it to someone in the announcer's stand. A moment later Mr. Dobranski began announcing the winners. David was watching Cassy and almost didn't notice that all four of his other students in the class received ribbons. Cassy's face didn't change as the results were read. She and the other three who did not place followed the winners out of the arena.

David started toward the barn, but the mother of one of his students stopped him to ask a question.

Cassy spotted him there as she came out of the arena. She wasn't disappointed. She hadn't expected to place. Very few people got a ribbon the first time they showed. But she'd proved to herself that she could do it. Even on a difficult horse, she could do it.

She was smiling when Maggie met her in the stall a few minutes later.

"I'm sorry," Maggie said. "She's never acted like that before. Are you okay?"

"Oh, yes. May I still show her in the Walk Trot Equitation class?" Cassy loosened the girth, but left it on.

"Sure—if you still want to." Maggie looked doubtful. "Do you think David will let you?"

"Actually, it doesn't matter. He's not my teacher, so I don't have to listen to him," Cassy said smugly.

"Oh, really?" David's voice came from behind Maggie. "Did I just get fired?"

Chapter Ten

" "I'll see you later," Maggie said before making a quick exit.

David leaned on the stall door, looking in. Cassy felt herself flushing and tried to ignore his presence. Idly she fingered a piece of leather on the saddle.

"I thought we agreed I was going to coach you," he said dryly, after several awkward moments of silence.

Cassy turned on him angrily. "Where was my *coach* when I had to switch horses and needed help this morning? You've been so busy helping everyone else that you weren't around when I needed you." She felt herself close to tears again but was determined not to let him see it.

David slipped inside the stall and stood facing her. He lifted her chin, forcing her to raise her eyes to meet his. "I didn't know you'd decided to show another horse," he said. "That wasn't a smart thing to do, with no preparation."

"We would have been fine if that dog hadn't gotten loose."

"Maybe. But you could have been hurt. That's what scared me."

"You were scared?" Cassy's eyes searched his.

"Darn right." He dropped his hand from her chin and stroked Lady absently. "You're a lot more to me than just a student. A lot more." He met Cassy's eyes again. "I'm sorry for getting mad at you. Apparently you had a more accurate assessment of the situation than I did."

"I was able to control her," Cassy said, meeting his eyes.

"I know that now. I was letting my fear for your safety cloud my judgment. Will you forgive me?"

Cassy melted at the look in his eyes. "On one condition."

"Which is?"

"You'll coach me now for the Equitation class."

David smiled warmly. "Of course." He glanced at his watch. "But we'd better get moving. That class is right after lunch break."

He reached over and tightened the girth again, and Cassy led the horse outside. He gave her a leg up, and they went together to an open area in the pasture.

For the next ten minutes Cassy alternately walked and trotted the horse under his direction, while he pointed out things she could do to improve. By the time her class was announced, both horse and rider were calm and confident.

David took a position near the announcer's stand to watch the class. The riders entered the arena. Cassy looked good—a definite improvement from her first class. Lady was calm, collected, and obedient. Their performance was flawless. They walked and trotted in both directions and lined up for the judge. This time they even backed correctly.

David waited anxiously for the results to be decided and conveyed to the announcer. There were only seven in the class, and Cassy definitely had a chance. He hadn't noticed any mistakes. Of course he hadn't paid as much attention to her competition. Actually, that wasn't good, he reminded himself. Two of his other students were in there too. He'd have to watch that— he shouldn't be showing favoritism.

Sixth place was announced, then fifth. Fourth went to one of David's other students. He held his breath. Third, and still Cassy had not been called.

"Second place to number 249, Miss Cassy Collins on Lady." David let out a whoop and joined several other people from the stable who clapped for her. He ran to the arena exit to meet her as she came out. He didn't even hear the winner of the class, as his attention was focused on Cassy.

Her face was beaming as she came out of the ring, exultantly holding her bright-red ribbon along with the reins. An equally beaming David met her outside the arena. He held the front of Lady's bridle as Cassy swung down from the saddle, and then he enveloped her in a bear hug.

"That was great," he said. "I'm so proud of you."

Cassy laughed with pure joy. "You wouldn't be a little bit prejudiced, would you?"

"Not at all," he said. "You always were a good student."

He put his arm around her shoulder as they headed toward the barn.

"I bet she was," Cassy heard a nearby voice whisper. She glanced at the source and saw a blonde standing nearby, whispering to another woman. They both gave her a disdainful look before turning away. Cassy's smile froze on her face.

"Ignore them," David said, feeling her stiffen. "We haven't done anything wrong."

They passed a couple of people from Greenwood, who saw the ribbon Cassy was clutching and called out congratulations. She tried to shrug off the overheard comment and enjoy her moment of glory.

When they reached the stall, Cassy started to remove the English saddle and bridle. David excused himself to go back to the show, since he still had students who were showing in later classes. Maggie joined her a few minutes later and together they brushed Lady and put on her own Western bridle, blanket, and saddle. Maggie had changed into a red-and-white fringed shirt. Over her jeans she wore black suede chaps held up by a leather belt with a shiny silver buckle. On her head was a black felt Stetson. She looked fantastic, but seemed unaware of it.

"You were great," she told Cassy. "You and Lady look good together."

"I like her," Cassy admitted. "If you ever decide to sell her, let me know." They were silent for a few minutes as they concentrated on the tasks at hand. Then Cassy asked, "Who placed first in that class? I was so excited to place that I didn't pay attention."

"Elizabeth Colton. She's been showing for a while. Actually, I think she should be moving up to canter classes."

"She doesn't take lessons here, does she?"

"I don't think so, but I've seen her before."

They finished preparing Lady for Maggie's class and led her outside the barn. "Thanks again," Cassy said after Maggie had mounted. "Now I'll be rooting for you." Maggie nodded and walked her horse off to practice.

A rumbling in her stomach reminded Cassy that she hadn't eaten anything since leaving home that morning. Tempting smells were coming from the portable hot-dog stand set up near registration. After checking on General again and getting some money from her purse, Cassy made her way to the concession stand.

While waiting her turn in line, Cassy couldn't help overhearing the conversation of the two women in front of her.

"I don't think it's fair," a heavily made-up woman in too-tight stretch pants was saying. "My daughter didn't place at all, and his girlfriend got second. He didn't even notice or stop to console Kitty, he was so busy congratulating his pet."

The younger woman who was with her opened her mouth to reply, but as she turned she noticed Cassy standing behind her, and abruptly shut her mouth again. She nudged her friend, who then glanced back and saw Cassy too.

Cassy forced a false smile to her face, realizing they were talking about David. Both women nodded at her and turned away. The younger one stepped up to place her order.

Suddenly losing her appetite, Cassy walked away. She found David watching the show from his former position by the announcer's stand. He smiled a greeting when she met him but immediately went back to concentrating on the class in progress. Cassy joined him in clapping for one of his students who placed.

Maggie's Western Pleasure class was next. "She looks great, doesn't she?" she commented to David.

"I've seen her do better," he answered. "Her hands are too stiff, and she's letting Lady hold her head too high."

"She's shown before, hasn't she?"

"Many times, since she was a kid. But this is the first time since losing Chad."

Cassy tried to focus on the other riders, but Maggie kept drawing her attention. She still thought she and Lady looked great. The class had ten riders who were all asked to walk, trot, and canter in both directions. Cassy couldn't spot any errors from any of them.

"How do you think she'll do?" she asked David as the riders lined up for the judge.

"Maggie?" At her affirmative nod, he frowned thoughtfully. "If I were judging, I'd give her third or fourth. The top places should go to that bay quarter horse and the Appaloosa. My two students did well but aren't experienced enough for the top places. They might get fourth and fifth."

The winners were announced. Cassy gazed at David in amazement. He had predicted correctly on the top five. Either he had ESP or he knew what he was doing.

David left her to greet his students as they came out. She went back to the barn and met Maggie there to congratulate her.

"What's wrong?" she asked, noticing that Maggie looked close to tears. "Third place is great."

"It's not that," Maggie said. "This is the first time Chad isn't here to congratulate me. We always came to shows together."

"I'm sorry," Cassy said, meaning it.

"Thanks. But I think I've had enough excitement for today. I'm going to head for home."

"Okay. Do you need any help?"

"Yes, I could use some assistance loading her. I'm not used to doing it alone yet."

Instead of going in the barn, they led Lady back to Maggie's horse trailer, where they quickly untacked her and replaced her bridle with her halter.

By the time they had finished and were ready to load, David arrived.

"You lead her in, and I'll close the back," he said to Maggie.

Since it appeared they didn't need her, Cassy stood by to watch.

Maggie led Lady around for a minute to calm her and then took her to the open back door of the small trailer. She threw the lead line over the horse's neck and said firmly, "Load in."

The horse obediently stepped up and walked into her stall in the trailer. The hay net was already in front waiting for her and she contentedly started munching while Maggie came around to the front window and attached the trailer tie to her halter.

David had closed the rear door and fastened the butt bar as soon as the horse was inside. He walked around the trailer once, checking to make sure everything was secure.

"Are you sure you don't want to wait for me?" he asked Maggie as she closed the trailer window and gathered up the last of her equipment.

"No, thanks. Unloading is the easy part. I'll be fine." She turned to face him, her lower lip quivering. "Thanks, David."

She reached out and hugged him, then quickly turned and got in her truck. "'Bye, Cassy," she said, noticing the young woman was still standing there, awkwardly watching.

"'Bye.'' Cassy watched as the truck and trailer slowly pulled out and left Greenwood behind. ''Do you think she'll be okay?'' she asked David as they started back toward the arena.

''I think so. I'll be leaving as soon as the last class is over. But I think she needs to find out that she can do it by herself.'' He noticed the doubtful look on Cassy's face.

''Don't worry—I'll check on her as soon as I get back.''

Cassy smiled gratefully. ''Okay.'' She was beginning to consider Maggie a friend and was glad her jealousy of the other woman was fading. They had too much in common to be adversaries.

''I think I'll head home too,'' she said. ''It's been a long day.''

''Okay.'' David looked into her eyes, and for a moment she thought he was going to kiss her. But several people came up to him as he took her hands in his. ''I'll see you later,'' he said, dropping her hands again and turning away.

Cassy went back to the barn to check on General one more time before leaving. He was doing fine, and she finished cleaning his stall and feeding him before going back to her car. The last class of the day was in the arena when Cassy finally climbed into her Honda. Most of the horse trailers were already gone or in the process of leaving. The crowds had dwindled. Most of the few people who remained were the ones who kept their horses at Greenwood.

Cassy looked back at the arena one more time as she waited for a large trailer to pull out ahead of her. Several students were clustered around David, and he didn't see her. She pursed her lips. He was a popular guy. She'd have to get used to sharing him. But at least she knew that he cared about her. She smiled as she thought about what he'd said about her earlier today. She meant a lot more to him than a student. He was a lot more to her than a teacher. A slight beep behind her made Cassy realize she was daydreaming. A glance in the rearview mirror showed the driver of the car behind her was the same woman who'd made the comment about her as she was coming out of her class. It figured.

She pulled out of the lot and down the drive. She wondered if other people felt that way too—those two ladies at the concession stand sure did. But she'd earned that ribbon! She'd even dropped out of David's clinic to prevent gossip like that. Well, if other people didn't like it, that was just too bad. Their personal relationship was no one's business but hers and David's. As long as they were happy, it shouldn't matter what other people thought.

Unfortunately, though, it did matter. She could tell David was embarrassed to show his affection toward her in front of his students. Would he ever be willing to proclaim her as his girlfriend? With a sigh, she turned toward home. It had been a very long day.

The next day and every other day that week Cassy went to work at the hospital and stopped briefly at Greenwood on her way home. On days she didn't see David at the stable, they talked on the phone later.

Christmas was rapidly approaching, and everyone at Greenwood was getting into the holiday spirit. Mr. Dobranski hung colored lights around the house and barn and put a huge Santa and sleigh with reindeer, including Rudolph, on the barn roof. His wife decorated the office with garlands and red bows and even hung mistletoe, well out of reach of the horses, above the doorway. Carols playing on the radio in the office could be heard all over the barn.

Cassy hummed "Joy to the World" along with the blaring radio as she entered the barn on Friday. It was her day off, and she'd already been to the mall to complete most of her Christmas shopping. After the hassle of fighting crowds and holiday traffic, she was especially happy to be back at the barn. She was satisfied with the gifts she'd found for her family and most of her friends, and she only had to buy for a few more special people, including David. Now she was ready for some relaxing time with her horse. His hoof was completely healed, and she could finally ride him again.

She stopped in the tack room long enough to pick up General's halter and a handful of grain, and then headed out the back of the barn to the pasture, where she found him peacefully grazing. He looked up when she called his name and then almost went back to eating the grass, but couldn't resist the urge to investigate the handful of sweet feed Cassy was holding out.

"Come on, General, I know you can't resist a bribe—especially if it's food," Cassy coaxed. She waited patiently while the big horse slowly wandered over, his eyes focused on the feed. As soon as he was close enough, she allowed him to eat out of her hand while she slipped the halter over his head with her other arm and snapped it closed. "You fall for it every time, don't you?" Cassy laughed as she affectionately scratched behind his ears, where she knew he liked it.

General tried to ignore her and reach down to graze some more, but Cassy tugged on the lead rope, and he obediently followed her to the gate. The other horses in the pasture were still busy grazing and didn't even look up as Cassy led General out and refastened the latch.

As she walked the horse back to the barn, Cassy looked toward the arena and saw that David's class was ending. She felt her heart beating a little faster at the sight of him. Even at a distance he had a distinctive air of power and authority. Unable to tear her eyes away, she stopped in the middle of the path and watched as he walked toward the barn.

General took advantage of her momentary lapse in concentration to grab a few last morsels of grass next to the path before his tugging on the lead alerted her that she needed to pay attention to what she was doing. With a determined pull, she brought him back and continued to the barn, where she put him in his stall.

The barn was bustling with activity as students came back from lessons and groomed and untacked their horses. Cassy had to wait for several people to leave the tack room before there was room for her to squeeze in to get General's things. She considered trying to find David first but decided he'd be busy in the office, for a while anyway.

As she stood in the doorway waiting, she was suddenly pulled off her feet into an embrace and kissed soundly on the lips. She staggered backward and almost fell as she was released. Her eyes widened in surprise.

"Richard!" She stared at Wendy's boyfriend in amazement.

"Just getting in the holiday spirit," he explained, grinning as he raised his eyes to the mistletoe over the door.

"Next time, practice your holiday spirit on your own girlfriend." The snarling voice was low but commanding. Cassy knew before she looked that it was David's.

He was standing in the aisle only a few feet behind Richard and had apparently seen him kiss her. His eyes were flashing in anger, his hands knotted in fists, though they hung at his side.

Cassy swallowed hard and looked from one man to the other. She'd never seen David so furious. He continued to glare at Richard. Even though his anger didn't seem to be directed at her, she was afraid to cross him.

Richard stared back at him for only a moment, then turned abruptly and walked away. The aisle quickly cleared of spectators, everyone wanting to stay clear of David's wrath.

Cassy waited a few moments, unsure what to do. David remained frozen in position, his eyes still watching the retreating Richard, as though making sure he was really leaving. While she watched, he relaxed visibly, his fists opening, his face softening. Finally he turned to Cassy and met her frightened eyes.

"He didn't mean anything," she said softly, not moving.

He looked searchingly into her eyes, his expression stern. Then wordlessly he turned back toward the office.

Cassy watched his retreat, puzzled. Was he angry at her? At Richard? When he reentered the office, she turned back to the tack room, which was now empty. She gathered her grooming equipment and walked slowly back to General's stall.

The big horse was contentedly munching hay but nuzzled her affectionately when she slipped into the stall. She started grooming him, her thoughts still on the incident with Richard. Did David think she'd done something to provoke it? She'd always been friendly with Richard but never flirted. Wendy was her friend, and both men knew it. Even if she'd been attracted to

Richard, she would never have shown it for Wendy's sake. And if he'd ever made a pass, she would certainly have resisted it. No, she'd done nothing to encourage the kiss. And Richard probably had just seized the opportunity for a little holiday fun. David was the one with the problem.

David reached the office and entered without knocking. He threw himself on the armchair and sat back, staring at the front of the desk. He was still there a few minutes later when Mr. Dobranski came in and seated himself behind the desk.

"Want to tell me what that little scene was all about?" the older man asked, drawing his thick brows together and folding his hands.

"Beats me . . . I've been asking myself the same thing." David shrugged and shook his head in confusion.

"Jealous, huh?"

David looked up quickly, as though surprised at the other man's perception. Then, seeing his unsmiling face, he nodded. "Yeah . . . I guess so." He paused a minute, wondering if he should explain further. Another glance at Mr. D.'s stern face convinced him he should. "I never told anyone this . . . but I caught Rhonda kissing another man. . . ."

The older man's fist hit the desk with a loud thump. "Doggone it, David, Cassy's not at all like Rhonda, and you know it. She's crazy about you, and you'd better do something about it before she realizes she's too good for you."

David looked up and met the other man's eyes. Mr. Dobranski's voice was serious, his tone critical. But his eyes were warm.

"I know." David ran his hand through his hair, lowering his eyes to stare at the desk again. "Guess I owe a few apologies, huh?"

"Guess so." The older man still didn't smile, but David knew him well enough to know he was pleased. Slowly he stood and headed out the office door, in search of Cassy, smiling when he heard the older man chuckle as soon as he thought David was out of earshot.

Cassy was still grooming General and getting more irritated by the minute. The more she thought about the scene with David and Richard, the angrier she became. She'd been the innocent party, so why should she be feeling guilty? She'd done nothing wrong! She marched back to the tack room for General's saddle and bridle. As she stepped out again, the saddle on one arm and holding up the bridle with the other, David suddenly stepped in front of her. Furious with him now, she simply stopped and glared.

He took her chin in his hand and kissed her lips.

With both hands full, she didn't try to resist. It was hard enough to stay upset with him with his warm lips touching hers.

He drew away first, his lip curling slightly in good humor, and raised his eyes upward to the mistletoe, which was above Cassy once again. "Holiday spirit is good—with the right person," he said, smiling.

Cassy brushed past him to head back to General's stall.

He followed her and took the saddle from her as she was lifting it to put it on the stall wall. He stood silently while she put on General's bridle and took the saddle pad from the top of the saddle and placed it on General's back. Then he placed the saddle on top of the pad already on the horse, and buckled up the girth on the far side for her.

She was still refusing to meet his eyes, going about her work and doing her best to ignore him.

He waited, finding her silent treatment more amusing than irritating.

Finally, as she picked up the reins to lead the horse out, he placed a restraining hand on her arm. "Wait."

She stopped, staring at the sawdust floor.

"Cassy, I'm sorry for blowing up." He waited while she raised her eyes to meet his. "I was jealous, that's all. Seeing another man kiss you made me go crazy for a minute. You're very special to me. Do you know that?"

She searched his eyes and saw only sincerity there. "You had no reason to be jealous," she whispered.

"Show me." His eyes were warm as he bent to kiss her. This time she responded with all the passion she was feeling. A wonderful warmth spread from her toes to the top of her head. Dropping the reins, she allowed her arms to go around him, loving the feel of his muscular chest against hers, his warm male scent filling her nostrils. How could he think she could ever be interested in another man's kiss? No other man had ever made her feel like this.

A throat being cleared alerted them that they were no longer alone. Pulling apart sheepishly, they looked into the smiling eyes of Mrs. Dobranski. "I can see you're busy, but my husband is waiting for you."

"Oh—my lesson! Sorry; tell him I'll be right there!" Cassy turned back to David. "Can you wait for me?"

"No, I've got lessons at Pine Haven." He took her hand. "But I still haven't made dinner for you. How about tonight?"

She accepted gladly, and they agreed on a time. Then

Cassy hurried out to the arena, and David headed back to Pine Haven.

After her lesson and taking care of General, Cassy called Wendy. Her friend had graduated from beauty school and was now working at a salon not far from Cassy's apartment. Cassy made an appointment for that afternoon.

Wendy was busy blow-drying an elderly woman's hair when Cassy arrived. "Have a seat. I'll be with you in a minute," she called to her friend.

Cassy perched on one of the pink chairs in front of the dryers. The women cocooned under the machines looked up long enough to nod at her before going back to reading their movie magazines.

Cassy smiled to herself. She hadn't been to a salon for a while, but things hadn't changed much. Wendy looked right at home among all the pink-and-mauve decor and mirrors. She picked up a book of sample hairstyles and started to flip through it.

After a few minutes, Wendy called to her that she was ready for her.

"So what's the occasion? Big date tonight?" she asked Cassy as she fastened a pink vinyl cape around her neck.

Cassy smiled shyly. "Dinner at David's house."

The blonde raised her eyebrows. "Ooh—sounds promising."

"I hope so," Cassy said. "We've only been out a couple of times, but I like him a lot."

"Just like?" Wendy lowered the chair and positioned Cassy in front of the sink.

Cassy smiled, not feeling a need to reply as Wendy began to wet and shampoo her hair. She closed her eyes and relaxed, enjoying the warm water and Wendy's gentle hands kneading her scalp. She inhaled deeply of the strawberry-scented shampoo.

Much too soon, the shampoo and rinse were finished. Wendy sat Cassy back up and briefly towel-dried her hair. They decided on a simple trim and blow-dry.

"Richard told me what happened this morning," Wendy said after combing out Cassy's hair. She started to pin up sections before pulling out her scissors. "It sounds to me like David feels more for you than he's letting on." Her eyes met Cassy's in the mirror, and then she started to clip.

Cassy could feel herself blushing. "I hope so . . . he says I'm important to him—but we hardly ever see each other except at Greenwood. I don't know if he even considers me his girlfriend."

Wendy paused for a minute and waved the scissors for emphasis as she looked at Cassy in the mirror. "Richard told me he apologized to him for overreacting. And he called you his 'girl'. It sounds to me like you two are an item." Her eyes twinkled as she started snipping again while Cassy watched in the mirror.

The trim took only a few minutes, and while Wendy blow-dried her hair, Cassy sat silently.

When Wendy started the finishing touches with a curling iron, Cassy renewed the conversation. "Do you think people at the stable are bothered by David dating me? I'd hate to cause problems for him." She was still remembering the comments she'd overheard at the horse show.

Wendy shrugged, then clipped the curler on a ringlet of hair. "Anybody who doesn't like it is in the minority. All of us who know you both are aware that David didn't give you any special treatment when you were in his clinic. If anything, he was harder on you 'cause he didn't want to admit he liked you.'' She released the hair and picked up another strand. ''David is a good teacher, and I think most of us would be grateful to have him stay in Orlando. Nobody I know would care if you're the reason.''

''Do you think I am?'' Cassy asked, disbelieving.

Wendy winked at her and leaned over to whisper in her ear conspiratorially. ''You'd know that better than I would, but the gossip around the barn is that the man is crazy about you. And if I were you, I'd grab him and hold on tight.''

Wendy finished adding gentle curls to her coiffure, and used a few puffs of hairspray to hold it in place. ''There,'' she said, stepping back to admire her handiwork. ''What do you think?''

Cassy looked at herself in the mirror. Her hair fell in soft waves on her shoulders. Gentle curls framed her face. She looked beautiful. ''Perfect . . . you're wonderful!'' she exclaimed.

Wendy smiled proudly. ''Let me know how David likes it,'' she said as Cassy paid her.

''I will; thanks so much.'' Cassy said good-bye to her friend and left the salon feeling very optimistic about her date.

Cassy took her time going home and getting ready for her dinner with David. She chose a dress to wear, this time a casual red knit to fit the season. After taking special care with her make up, she donned the dress and added a pair of dress boots. They'd be functional tonight with the weather dipping below freezing.

She stood in front of the mirror and decided she approved of the final product. She'd never looked better. She'd heard that being in love made a person look radiant. Could that be true? *Yes,* she smiled at herself. She was in love with David Carlyle. And whatever happened later would depend on if he loved her too.

He still hadn't said the words . . . but neither had she. Still, she knew he cared a lot about her. Surely he wouldn't let a kiss from another man, especially an innocent one under the mistletoe, bother him if he didn't consider her his woman.

She leaned dreamily against the wall as she remembered when he'd told her he was moving to Orlando for good. He'd said, "Everything I want is here now." Did that mean love as well?

It was time to go. Soon she'd be with him again.

Cassy hunched her shoulders and pushed her free hand deep into the pocket of her coat as she opened the car door and immediately felt the onslaught of cold air hit her. It seemed to be even colder than when she'd left her apartment, but maybe it just seemed that way after sitting in the warm car with her coat on.

She climbed out quickly and slammed the car door, then tucked her purse under her arm and headed for David's trailer. She was beginning to wish she'd worn pants, as the cold wind whipped her stockinged legs. Good thing she could park close to the door. She skipped up the two steps and rapped twice on the door. It was opened almost immediately, and she slipped inside, at once noticing the wonderful aroma of beef Burgundy that greeted her along with the warm interior air.

David looked dashing in a blue pullover sweater that matched his eyes exactly. He was smiling sympathetically as he shut the door and took her freezing-cold hand in his warm one. "You look great," he said, gazing at her appreciatively. Cassy felt warmer already.

"Come on," he said, pulling her toward the kitchen. "You need some hot apple cider."

"Perfect," she admitted, gladly accepting the mug he handed her when they entered the kitchen. Her hand froze in place halfway to her mouth, however, as she spotted the slim brunette setting the table in the dining area.

Chapter Eleven

Maggie saw her at the same moment, and her smile was innocent and friendly as she came toward them. "Let me take your coat," she told Cassy, as though she were the hostess.

Trying not to show her surprise at Maggie's presence, Cassy put her cider on the counter and slipped out of her coat. Wordlessly she handed it to the other woman and watched as she took it toward the living room, then turned expectantly raised eyes toward David.

"I hope you don't mind that I invited Maggie to join us for dinner," David said in a voice too low to carry to the next room. "She came by earlier when I was cooking—and I do owe her several dinners by now. I'd like you to get to know her better anyway."

Cassy forced a bright smile to her lips. "Of course not. I'd like that too." She picked up her mug and took a sip of the warm sweet liquid, while leaning her back comfortably against the counter.

David took a moment to check under the lid of the pot from which the wonderful aroma was wafting.

160

"Almost ready," he said. "Why don't you ladies go in the living room and relax while I finish up?" He picked up a spoon and lifted the lid of the pot again.

"Are you sure we can't help?" Maggie asked from the doorway.

"Nope. I don't want you to learn my secrets." He winked at Cassy and turned back to the pot.

"Okay, then." Maggie poured herself a fresh cup of cider, and the two of them retired to the living room, taking their mugs with them. Cassy sat primly on one end of the couch, and Maggie took the chair across from her, sprawling comfortably across the arms.

Maggie spoke first. "What do you think of David's new horse?"

"I think he's wonderful!" Cassy's smile was sincere. She couldn't help liking this pretty brunette. It was hard to resent someone who seemed so genuinely friendly. If Maggie were interested in David, she should be jealous of Cassy, but she certainly didn't seem to mind sharing him.

They talked amiably about horses and show jumping, and by the time David came in to tell them dinner was ready, they were chatting like old friends.

"I knew my two favorite ladies would get along fine," he said, poking his head into the room. "And now, you two are in for a treat."

Both women rose to their feet and followed the aroma. "I hope this evening won't end with a trip to the Emergency Room for food poisoning," Maggie teased.

"Don't worry, I know the staff there and can get us in quickly," Cassy added, trying to keep from laughing.

David made a face at both of them. "You two had better bite your tongues or I'll throw you out and eat it all myself!"

"Okay, we'll take our chances." Maggie laughed.

David made a show of pulling out two chairs and seating the women on opposite sides of the square table before taking a third chair between them.

"This looks wonderful," Cassy admitted, surveying the meal laid out on the table. A delicious-looking salad sat before them, as well as three heaping plates of beef Burgundy over noodles, and a bowl of freshly baked garlic bread.

"You called a caterer, right?" Maggie asked, in mock disbelief.

"I can still throw you out, you know." David pretended to glare at her, but Maggie ignored him, unfolded her napkin, and placed it in her lap.

The meal tasted as good as it looked, and the conversation was equally pleasant as they all shared amusing stories about horses and horse people. Cassy found that she was enjoying Maggie's company almost as much as David's. The good-natured kidding between them kept the mood light and her mind off what might happen later. Only a few times did she feel slight pangs of jealousy when David met Maggie's eyes over an apparently private joke.

When all three had emptied their plates, the two women readily admitted that David was as good a cook as he had claimed. It was mutually agreed to wait for dessert, since they were already full.

The women cleared the table while David made coffee. They insisted on helping clean up, and since he had no dishwasher David didn't put up much of a fight. It was a bit crowded with all three of them in the tiny kitchen, but they had fun.

Finally, the last dish washed and dried, David suggested dessert.

"Thanks, but I'm kind of tired," Maggie said. "I appreciate your inviting me—it was fun. See you tomorrow." She bundled into her coat and then disappeared into the darkness outside.

"She's really nice," Cassy said when the door closed. "I'm glad you invited her."

David looked into her eyes. "You're very special. Do you know that?"

Cassy smiled happily at him. "What's for dessert?"

David was tempted to say, "Me," but checked himself. Instead he said, "Strawberry cheesecake."

"Mmm." Cassy licked her lips. "I'll pour the coffee." She retrieved their cups from the counter and poured while David cut two slices of cheesecake and placed them on plates. Together they carried their dessert into the living room. Cassy sat on the couch while David settled on the chair across from her.

"Don't tell me you made this too?" Cassy took a tentative bite.

"No, I have to admit I didn't. Maggie brought it over this afternoon. That's when I invited her to stay for dinner."

"It's delicious." Cassy was eating slowly, savoring each bite. She looked up to find David's eyes on her and paused. David took their plates and laid them on the coffee table. Her heart was beginning to race madly.

His eyes never leaving her face, David perched on the edge of the couch next to her and reached behind her to draw her over into his arms. She melted into them, her own going automatically around his neck and shoulders. Her hand found the cluster of curls at the base of his neck, and she marveled at the coarse, yet soft, feel of his hair between her fingers. His pleasant male scent filled her nostrils, and she inhaled deeply.

Their lips met, warm, moist, and sweet. They kissed hungrily, fervently. Cassy felt herself forgetting everything else around her.

David too was lost in the moment. Neither noticed the sound of running footsteps coming up the path until they were followed by a series of pounding knocks on the front door.

"What the—" David drew away, cursing under his breath. He leaped to his feet almost immediately, an angry frown creasing his face as he strode across the room. He threw open the door to reveal a shivering Maggie.

"I'm sorry, David," she said, looking genuinely apologetic.

David didn't wait for her to explain, but pulled her quickly inside and shut the door again before turning expectantly back to her. "What is it?"

"I think some of the horses are sick. I wouldn't bother you if it was just mine, but Ebony is down too." She sounded almost hysterical.

"Okay, let's go take a look." David was instantly concerned. He reached in the closet by the door for a heavy jacket.

Cassy had followed him. She reached for her coat too, and started to put it on.

David gave her a critical look. "That won't be warm enough. We may be out there a while. Wait. I have an idea." He disappeared toward the bedroom.

Maggie turned her apologetic eyes toward Cassy. "I'm really sorry to interrupt your evening. . . . "

"It's okay. If you need help, we'd want to know." Cassy met the other woman's eyes and saw she was really frightened.

David returned with a pair of coveralls and a wool

hat. "Here, put these on. They'll be big, but you can roll them up. Your legs will freeze in those stockings."

Cassy took them gratefully. He was right. She hadn't planned on being outside very much tonight. The coveralls would protect her dress too. "Okay, I'll meet you in the barn," she said, shrugging back out of her coat.

David gave her a grim nod and opened the door. Another gust of cold air rushed in as he and Maggie slipped out.

Left alone, Cassy shivered and put on the coveralls. Apparently they were David's. She could smell his after-shave as she held them open. He was right about their being a bit large. She grinned as she held out her arms and looked at the extra length extending to her fingertips. The legs covered her boots completely. However, it took only a few extra minutes to roll them up. Then she put her coat on over them and slipped the wool hat on her head. Feeling a bit like the abominable snowman, she decided she was ready.

This time only her face and hands felt the cold when she opened the door. Although it was dark out, there was enough of a moon to see the path to Maggie's house and the barn behind it. She walked quickly, her boots crunching in the gravel.

She was amazed at all the night sounds that surrounded her as she made her way to the barn. Thousands of tiny insect voices mingled with the deep croaks of bullfrogs and the pleasant, but lonely, call of the whip-poorwill. Somewhere in the distance she could hear the hoot of an owl.

The barn lights were on, but the doors were closed to keep in the warmth. Cassy unlatched them and slipped inside. Several of the horses nickered softly and thrust their noses at her. She ignored them and headed straight to Ebony's stall, which she knew to be at the far end, well away from Maggie's mares.

But the dull-eyed, listless horse she saw there bore little resemblance to the prancing steed she'd seen before. He was lying down in his stall with David squatting at his head, checking the color of his gums.

"Looks like colic," David said, barely glancing at her. "Maggie is calling the vet. Can you help me take his temp?"

"Sure. I'm a nurse, remember?" She entered the stall and took the large thermometer with a string attached that David handed her.

"I don't suppose he can hold it under his tongue?" she asked in an attempt at humor.

David smiled grimly. "I don't think so."

He stayed at the horse's head, holding his halter and talking softly to him, while Cassy positioned herself behind the stallion. It seemed so strange to see this huge animal lying so docile and helpless. He made no attempt to resist as Cassy lifted his tail and inserted the rectal thermometer.

"This isn't exactly the romantic evening I had planned," David said ruefully, as they sat in the stall waiting for the temperature to register.

Cassy grinned good-naturedly. "Now I know why you invited a nurse." Their eyes met, and Cassy felt warm all over in spite of the cold outside.

She checked her watch and then withdrew the thermometer and read it. "101," she said aloud, raising her eyebrows.

"Good—that's normal for horses," David explained. They both stood up as the sound of footsteps alerted them that Maggie was returning.

"Dr. West can't come for at least an hour," she said,

breathless from hurrying. "The sudden drop in temperature is causing colic all over the county. His partner is even farther away. But he said we could give them each two cc's of Banamine if they seem to be in pain."

"Okay." David took the news calmly. "Do you have syringes and the medicine?"

Maggie nodded. "I'll get them." She turned and walked briskly away.

David turned back to Cassy. "Looks like your nursing skills will come in handy. Would you like to give the injections?"

Cassy hesitated. "I've never given one to a horse before. . . . "

"It's simple. I'll show you."

Maggie returned with several needles and syringes, some alcohol wipes, and a vial of Banamine. David took one of each and handed them to Cassy. After raising her eyebrows in surprise at the size of the needle, she opened the wipe and cleaned the top of the bottle. Then she screwed the needle onto the syringe and removed the plastic needle cover with her mouth. "Two cc's?" she asked between clenched teeth, turning to Maggie. At the other woman's affirmative nod, she pulled back the syringe to draw in two cc's of air, then plunged it into the bottle and drew out the same amount of medicine. She put the needle cover back on and turned to David.

He was looking at her approvingly. "Good job. I'll give it to Ebony." Willingly, she surrendered the prepared syringe to him and watched as he deftly found the proper place on the horse's neck muscle and cleaned it. However, instead of inserting the complete set of needle and syringe as she always did on human patients, he separated them and, giving a slight pat to

Ebony's neck, plunged in the needle only. Then he reattached them and finished the injection.

"I'm impressed," she admitted.

David shrugged modestly. "Think you can do Maggie's horses? I need to start walking Ebony."

Although she would have preferred to stay with David, Cassy agreed. She and Maggie moved down the aisle to a bay mare that was obviously in the same shape as David's stallion. They set to work preparing and giving the injection, barely noticing when David got Ebony to his feet and led him outside. Then they did the same with a third horse, an Appaloosa mare. After the injections, they coaxed the horses to their feet and led them outside to join David in walking a large circle around the pasture.

There was just enough moonlight to see where they were going. After the relative warmth of the barn, the cold outside air was bone chilling. Cassy's feet and hands quickly reached a state of numbness. It was impossible to talk to one another above all the night sounds, so they simply plodded on, three cold people leading three resisting horses. They continued on around and around, talking softly to the horses and keeping them moving. They had no real concept of time, but it seemed well over an hour before the sight of approaching headlights alerted them that the vet was arriving at last. Gladly, they all trooped back to the barn and put the horses in their respective stalls.

Dr. West, a short balding man who appeared to be in his fifties, strode purposely up to the first mare's stall, obviously not willing to waste time with cordialities.

"What's her temp?" he asked brusquely, pulling out a stethoscope and listening intently to the mare's belly.

Maggie told him and added that they'd given her the

Banamine. He nodded, then stood and addressed David. "Are the others any worse?"

David shook his head. "No, we've been walking all of them. They all seem to be better." The mare was making no attempt to lie down now.

"Good. I think it's a simple case of colic from not drinking enough water. When it gets too cold, they don't like it. I'll tube them all with mineral oil and warm water. Don't give them any hay or feed until tomorrow night. Okay?" His faded blue eyes flicked briefly to each of them, and then he turned toward Maggie. "I need buckets of warm water—three of them."

Without a word Maggie left to get them. The vet went back to his truck to get his equipment, leaving David and Cassy alone in the aisle outside the stall. For the first time since they'd come in, David really looked at her.

"Are you okay?" he asked, alarmed. She was extremely pale, what little he could see of her under the bundle of clothes he'd made her wear. Her face had a frightened expression he'd never seen on her before.

"I don't feel very well," she admitted. She wasn't sure what it was she was feeling. At first she'd thought it was just the cold and fatigue setting in. After all, they'd been out there walking the horses for what seemed like forever. But now her stomach was churning. Surely seeing a sick horse wouldn't affect her like that?

"I'm taking you inside," David decided immediately. He'd never seen her look like this. Something was definitely wrong.

She nodded, and then as he moved to take her hand, she suddenly felt herself go limp . . . and everything went black.

David scooped her up and carried her down the hall.

As he passed a worried-looking Maggie, he called out to her that Cassy was sick and he was taking her to the house, which was closer than his trailer. She nodded and continued filling a water bucket.

Cassy started to come to as she felt herself being lowered onto a bed. Groggily she watched through half-closed eyes as David stripped off her boots, and she offered no resistance as he removed her coat. Suddenly a wave of nausea hit her and she forced herself to consciousness and looked frantically for the closest bathroom. Spotting a doorway that looked promising, she made a dash for it. She made it just in time. She was dimly aware of David appearing next to her, placing his comforting arms on her shoulder and handing her a damp washcloth.

"Are you sure you'll be okay?" David was torn between wanting to give her some privacy and concern for her.

She forced herself to smile weakly. "Guess I finally caught the flu that's been going around the hospital. Just let me rest a while . . . I'll be fine."

"Well . . . okay. I'd better see if Maggie's doing okay. You're sure it's just the flu?" He was helping her back to the bed.

She nodded weakly, sinking onto the edge of the mattress.

"Okay, I'll be back as soon as I check on Maggie." He still looked undecided as he turned and walked out. A minute later Cassy heard the front door shut.

She carefully removed the coveralls and let them drop to the floor before crawling under the warm covers of the bed and falling almost instantly asleep.

By the time David got back to the barn, the vet had finished administering the warm water and oil to all three horses and they were all looking much better. He was giving some last instructions to Maggie when David entered the barn. After she assured him that everything was fine and she'd be in shortly, David hurried back to the house.

He found Cassy sound asleep, her hair spread like a mahogany mane around her face. Tenderly, he tucked the covers around her, resisting the urge to kiss the sprinkle of freckles over her nose. Her breathing was shallow but regular now, and her color was starting to come back.

He sank wearily on the chair near the bed, enjoying the view of her peacefully sleeping. She looked like an angel serenely resting like that. Thank goodness she seemed to be okay. He didn't know what he'd do if something happened to her.

As he sat there in Maggie's bedroom watching Cassy sleep, David suddenly realized the depth of his feelings for her. He had just seen this woman at her worst, and still he thought she was the most beautiful thing he'd ever seen! He shook his head in amazement. He was in love with Cassy Collins. He laid his head back against the chair, exhausted. He'd have to tell her first thing in the morning. . . .

Maggie's hand was gently shaking him. "It's morning, David. Go on home, I'll stay with her."

He was instantly awake. A quick glance at his watch told him it was almost six o'clock. "Darn. I have a meeting in a couple of hours." He looked at Cassy, still sleeping. "Okay, I'd better try to catch a shower before I have to go. What about you, did you get any sleep?"

She nodded. "I napped on the couch in between checking on the horses. Believe me, it's a lot more comfortable than that chair."

"Are the horses okay?" He'd almost forgotten about them in his concern for Cassy.

"Fine. And Cassy will be too."

He ran a hand through his rumpled hair. "Okay, I'll see you later. What a night, huh?"

Maggie followed him to the door and closed it quietly behind him. Yes, it had been quite a night, and she was glad it was over.

Cassy woke two hours later to find herself in Maggie's bed. She still felt weak, but the nausea was gone. She pulled back the covers and swung her bare feet to the floor. Someone must have removed her stockings. At least she was still wearing her dress. She blushed all over again, remembering how ill she'd been. David would probably never want to see her again!

She found Maggie asleep on the couch. While she debated what to do, Maggie slowly opened her eyes. "Oh, good—you're awake."

Maggie sat up, blinking sleepy eyes. "How about some hot tea?"

"Don't go to any trouble for me; you've already given up your bed." Cassy sank onto the nearest chair, feeling very weak.

"That's okay. I've been feeling kind of queasy myself. Tea is all I can usually handle in the morning." She rose and walked into the kitchen.

Still feeling too ill to argue, Cassy waited until Maggie returned with two cups of steaming tea and gratefully took one from her. "Do you think you're catching the flu too?" she asked.

Maggie shrugged. "Could be. I've been feeling awfully tired too—even before I had a reason to."

She filled Cassy in on the condition of the horses, and explained that David had gone to a meeting. They finished their tea in silence, both too tired for more conversation.

After drinking her tea, Maggie felt better and went out to feed the horses. Since Cassy didn't have to work that day, Maggie convinced her to stay there and rest.

Cassy took a long nap. Feeling refreshed, she told Maggie she wanted to go home, and convinced the other woman that she was well enough to drive herself.

Back in her own apartment, Cassy fixed herself a light lunch and called the Dobranskis to ask them to take care of General. By then, she was totally exhausted again and fell fast asleep on her couch, not rousing until morning.

When she awakened at her usual time, she felt totally back to normal, so she dressed and went to work as usual.

Luckily it was a slow day at the hospital, because Cassy wore herself out very quickly. Unable to face cafeteria food, she settled for tea and toast for lunch. By the end of her shift she was exhausted. Too tired to even take care of General, she called the Dobranskis and asked them to do it for her again.

David called several times over the next few days. Although he offered to come and see her, she assured him that she had everything she needed and just wanted to get some rest. He told her Maggie hadn't been feeling very well either, and he was trying to help her out in addition to all his regular work.

By her third day back at work, Cassy was fully recovered. She drove straight from work to Greenwood. David was there, but he was in the middle of a lesson, so she didn't interrupt. Instead she busied herself taking care of General. The horse was in dire need of a good grooming. After brushing and feeding him and cleaning his stall, she watched the remainder of David's lesson.

When the class was over, Cassy waited patiently while some of the students lingered, clustering around David, asking questions.

It wasn't hard to watch him. He was clad as usual in tan breeches, a blue tailored shirt, and the black knee-high boots. Although most of his body was covered by his clothing, she could see the muscles rippling under his shirt as he used his hands in talking. A tuft of black curly hair was visible at his neck.

The last of the students were leaving, so Cassy ambled over to the fence to meet David as he came out. His smile was warm and welcoming as he met her eyes, though fatigue lines marked his face.

"Hi, Cassy, feeling better?" He took her hand and lightly brushed her lips with his own.

"Much. I feel ready to rejoin the living." Her eyes were shining with happiness.

"Good. I've missed you." Still holding her hand he started walking toward the barn and she fell into step with him. "I need to talk to you—but not here. Can you come out to Pine Haven tomorrow?"

"Yes, it's my day off, but—"

"Good. I'll see you tomorrow then." David dropped her hand, and, looking distractedly at his clipboard, strode away.

Cassy stopped and waited, feeling as though she had just been dismissed. She watched as he continued on toward the office.

But before he reached it, Maggie's pickup truck pulled up. Cassy saw David turn at the sound of his name and rush to meet Maggie as she hopped out of the truck and ran toward him. Apparently she had good

news, because her face was shining as she spoke to
him. Cassy couldn't hear what they said but she
watched in dismay as David embraced the other woman
and lifted her off her feet to twirl her around.

A jealous rage was creeping up inside Cassy. Unable
to watch anymore, she turned abruptly and walked all
the way around the back of the barn to avoid seeing
them again. They were both out of sight by the time
she reached her car. She jumped inside and slammed
the door closed, still seeing Maggie in David's arms—
where *she* wanted to be.

By the time she got home, Cassy's temper had
reached a low simmer. She was trying to think of a
logical explanation for David's behavior. He had
seemed glad to see her. But he had sounded serious
when he said he wanted to talk to her.

What if he wanted to break off their relationship?
He was still spending a lot of time with Maggie. Maybe
he had fallen in love with her after all! Maggie was a
great person—Cassy even liked her herself. How could
she blame David for falling for her?

Cassy fixed herself a frozen dinner and then let it
grow cold as she picked at it with her fork. She couldn't
shake the feeling of foreboding that tomorrow she'd
find that her happiness in falling in love with David
was short lived. Yes, she knew now she was in love
with him. She'd been in love with him almost the whole
time she'd known him—almost three months now. But
she'd never told him. Maybe that was best. If he didn't
love her too there was no point in letting him know
how she felt and how he'd hurt her.

Cassy didn't sleep much that night. Restlessly she
tossed and turned, and when she did doze, she kept

having haunting dreams that she was in David's arms. But then he'd push her away and run to Maggie.

Finally at dawn, she fell into a sound sleep which lasted several hours. She woke only mildly refreshed.

It was two days before Christmas. The radio was broadcasting happy Christmas carols as Cassy came out of the shower and dressed in jeans and her favorite pink sweater. Not wanting to prolong the agony of not knowing where she stood with David, she decided to skip breakfast and head straight out to Pine Haven.

She spotted him as she pulled into the parking area in front of the log cabin. He was wearing jeans and a sweatshirt and carrying a large box. As she got out of her car, Cassy saw Maggie open the front door and hold it open while David carried the box through. Then she closed the door, and, spotting Cassy, hurried toward her.

"Go on in. David's in the house unpacking," she called to Cassy as soon as she was within earshot.

"Unpacking?" Cassy asked, puzzled.

"Yes. Didn't he tell you? He's moving in today."

Chapter Twelve

Maggie had passed Cassy but was continuing to walk toward her truck.

"No. . . . " Cassy suddenly felt her knees going weak.

"Well, it was kind of sudden . . . you see, I found out yesterday that I'm pregnant and . . . well, David will tell you all about it. I have to go now." Maggie was obviously in a hurry as she climbed in her truck and sped off without looking back.

Cassy stared after the truck in shock. This was what David wanted to tell her? That he was moving in with Maggie—and worse yet, that she was carrying his baby? How long ago did this happen? Had he been with Maggie the whole time he was seeing her?

In a daze of pain, she walked back to her car and got in. She sat staring at the steering wheel without seeing it and didn't even notice when David came back out the door and called her name.

David hurried over to her car. When she didn't acknowledge him, he jerked open the door. "What's the matter?" he demanded.

Cassy looked at him with glazed eyes. "Are you moving in with Maggie?" she asked in a toneless voice.

David put his hands on his hips. "I'm moving into the house, but Maggie—"

"Is pregnant?" She spat out the word as though she hated the sound.

David stared at her accusing eyes. "Wait a minute . . . you don't think I—" He paused as he realized what she was thinking. "Cassy, I thought you knew me better than that." He searched her expression while his eyes darkened in anger and pain. Cassy remained silent. She bit her lip and put the key in the ignition. David slammed the door shut again and turned abruptly back toward the house.

Cassy put the car in reverse and then sped away, not really knowing where she was going, just that she had to get away.

When she'd gone, David went back to the trailer for more of his things. After a couple of trips, he had it all.

Maggie returned a short while later to find him slouched in a chair, drinking a beer. "Hi," she said brightly. "I got my ticket. I can leave this afternoon."

"That's good." David nodded, staring at his beer can.

"What's wrong? Did you explain to Cassy?"

David crushed the can with his hand. "Cassy thinks I'm moving in with you to raise *our* baby."

"What? What did you tell her?"

"Nothing. She reached her own conclusion."

Maggie sat on the edge of the couch and stared at him. "You didn't explain?"

He shook his head, not looking at her.

"David Carlyle, you are an unfeeling jerk!"

He raised surprised eyebrows and finally looked at Maggie.

"You heard me. What is she supposed to think if all she knows is that I'm pregnant and you're moving into my house? Did you tell her you love her yet?"

"No, but she knows how I feel."

"Does she?"

David looked back at the crushed can in his hand. "Well . . . maybe not."

"I'd say definitely not." Maggie got up and went toward the kitchen. "Want another beer?" she called over her shoulder.

"No." David rose and followed her, tossing the can in the basket by the door. He picked up the phone.

"I have packing to do," Maggie said smiling knowingly. "Tell her I said hello." She took a can of soda from the refrigerator and disappeared down the hall.

Almost as though it knew the way itself, Cassy's car got her to Greenwood. Barely aware of where she was, Cassy got out and went to tack up General. She knew she didn't want to go home. She couldn't face the empty apartment. A ride by herself was what she needed. Getting back to nature, away from everything. And everyone.

She went about the business of getting General ready. The few people she passed were busy doing their own chores and didn't seem to notice her zombielike appearance.

As Cassy led General past the office on their way out of the barn, Mrs. Dobranski called out to her to wait. She stopped and checked her girth while the older woman came out to speak to her.

"David called to see if you were here. He wants to talk to you. I can hold General while you come to the phone."

"No, thanks, I don't need to talk to him," Cassy said in a choking voice. "Tell him to enjoy his life with Maggie and their baby!" Unable to meet the other woman's eyes, she picked up the reins and continued out, mounting as soon as she was outside and heading down the trail.

"Wait! What do you mean, their baby . . . Cassy!" Mrs. Dobranski tried in vain to get Cassy to stop, then stamped back into the office to find out what was going on.

Cassy continued on the trail, picking up a trot once she reached the shelter of the trees, and taking a canter as soon as she came to the clearing. It was a beautiful winter day. The sky was sunny, though the air was cold. But it was wasted on Cassy. She cantered the horse on and on, trying to forget the pain in her heart.

Finally, she turned down the path to the lake. There she had to take it slow, aware enough of her surroundings to realize she didn't want to endanger General. After walking to the edge of the pond, she dismounted and tied General to a branch of the same tree where she and David had tied their horses when they'd picnicked there. Leaving the horse to munch on what little winter grass was left, she walked slowly to the edge of the pond and sat there hugging her knees. Finally alone, with only General to hear, Cassy allowed the pain to wash over her.

At first only a few choking tears rolled down her cheeks. But as she tasted the salty liquid touching the corners of her mouth, suddenly the dam broke and the cleansing tears rolled easily, pouring out all the sadness of what could have been. She thought about the day she'd met David, when she thought he was someone's husband. If only he had been married! She would never have allowed herself to fall in love with him—to even think of him as anything but her teacher.

If only she could have thought of him as just a teacher. She had learned so much from him—but it had been so hard to concentrate on the lessons and forget how good he looked!

And gradually she'd gotten to know him as more than just an attractive instructor. He was kind and thoughtful and cared about children and animals. He'd been through a lot of pain, but he'd come through it. He'd been so understanding when she was sad. Remembering how he'd held her when her patient died brought on a new wave of tears, because she wanted nothing more than to have him holding her like that again now. But if he was holding her now she wouldn't have a reason to be crying!

She'd given up her riding lessons with him—where she was learning so much—so that he wouldn't have to be seen dating his student. And all the time he just wanted someone to be seen with while he was secretly seeing his friend's widow. His friend who was barely in the grave!

And to think she'd been worried about Rhonda! Why should he go back to his ex when he had a perfectly willing woman right next door, cooking for him, taking care of his horse, and apparently a whole lot more? She'd been such a fool!

At last her tears were spent. Cassy had been so involved in her grief, that she didn't notice when General got tired of reaching for the few sprigs of brown grass and managed to untie himself and walk away.

As her thoughts turned away from sadness, Cassy began to get angry. By the time the last of her tears had fallen, she was asking herself why she was wasting her tears on a man who would treat her that way.

She rose and walked along the edge of the pond, stooping to pick up pebbles and toss them in the water, watching as they formed little ripples when they hit the water.

She didn't notice as a man on horseback came out of the woods and jumped down off his mount, until his running footsteps slowly permeated her consciousness. She whirled to face him just as he reached her and grabbed her shoulder with one hand, the other still holding the horse.

"David!" Her tear-streaked face was red and swollen.

"Are you okay?" He frowned into her face.

She pulled away from him and turned away. "Of course."

"You don't look it." He stayed behind her.

"I was upset. But I'm okay now," she lied. Seeing him again was the last thing she needed.

He reached for her shoulders and turned her around to face him, though her eyes were focused on the ground. "When General came back to the barn without you, I was worried sick! Don't you know you shouldn't ride out alone?"

She nodded, still not wanting to look at him. He dropped his hands and thrust them in his pockets, as he spun away from her. "Do you have any idea how many people are concerned about you right now? When you wouldn't talk to me I came out to Greenwood. Mrs. D. was telling me she thought you were upset when you left, and then General came back without you. . . . " He shook his head as he continued. "I've never been so scared in my life! I jumped on General and tore out of there like greased lightning. I imagine they'll send a search party out as soon as they get some more horses saddled up.'' He turned back toward her and found her watching him through tear-filled eyes.

''I'm sorry. I didn't realize General got loose—I tied him to the tree.'' David was tying him there again—securely this time.

''You didn't fall, then?'' He still looked concerned.

''No. Not this time.'' She was reminded of the time they'd met. She bent and picked up a large rock and hurled it into the pond.

''I imagine you were wishing that was my head,'' he said dryly from behind her.

Without turning she said, ''Don't I have reason to?''

''No—not if you knew the truth.''

''Which is?'' She still faced the water, not trusting herself to turn around and look at him.

''Sit down, and I'll explain it all to you.''

''Just tell me if you're moving in with Maggie.'' She stayed where she was.

''I was afraid that's what you were thinking.'' David reached around her and squeezed her back to his chest, burying his face in her hair. ''I'm moving into the house—but Maggie's moving out. I suppose you think the baby is mine?''

She nodded, her eyes filling with tears again.

''Oh, Cassy, don't you know me better than that!'' He let go of her and stepped back.

She spun around, new hope springing to her eyes. ''Then who . . . ?''

''Chad! She must have gotten pregnant right before he was killed. She never suspected she might be having his baby because they'd tried for a long time. She attributed all the symptoms to the shock of his death. But the doctor confirmed it yesterday. She's thrilled, and I'm happy for her. I can't believe you had so little faith in me—in our relationship. . . . '' He strode away from Cassy and reached for General's reins. ''We'd better be heading back.''

''Wait, David.'' Cassy was starting to feel alive again. But now he was angry with her! ''Please . . . tell me the rest.''

He hesitated, then dropped the reins again as he turned a searching gaze back to her. Her red-rimmed eyes were shining now. He reached out and brushed her hair away from her face. This was the woman he loved. He had to tell her the rest of it. She was suffering needlessly.

''Maggie is going to spend the holidays with her family and stay with them till the baby is born. She's not sure what she wants to do after that. But I've offered to lease the ranch. I was hoping you'd marry me and help me run it.'' His eyes locked with hers, and he smiled as he saw them widen in surprise and then joy.

''Well,'' he said teasingly, ''I just proposed. Are you going to give me an answer now or keep me in suspense?''

Cassy's eyes were filling again, this time from gladness. ''Yes!'' she said happily. ''Yes, yes, yes!'' She threw her arms around him and laughed as he grabbed her waist and spun her around just as he'd spun Maggie the day before. It felt much better to be on the receiving end!

After twirling around several times, they both collapsed, laughing on the ground. David's happy eyes met her shining ones, and he smiled. ''I was going to save this for Christmas,'' he said, reaching into his pocket and pulling out a small jewelry box. ''But I think you should have it now.'' He handed it to her and she slowly opened it, revealing a perfect diamond ring.

''It's beautiful!'' She gasped.

Carefully he reached in and removed it from the box, then slowly slipped it on her finger. A perfect fit.

''Oh, David, I love you.'' Cassy started crying all over again.

Still holding her hands, he searched her eyes for signs of doubt. ''Will you mind cutting down your hours at the hospital?'' he asked. ''I could hire someone else to help me—but I'd rather have you.''

Cassy smiled through her tears, as she shook her head. ''I'd love it.''

He leaned over and kissed her, on the lips this time. Immediately all thoughts of weeping fled as she responded with all the warmth she was feeling. A fire was spreading from the tips of her toes through her body like wildfire.

''Whoa,'' he said, smiling tenderly as he drew away. ''There'll be plenty of time for that later. Right now we'd better get back before the search party gets here.''

She knew he was right. Together they rose, and she followed him to the tree and waited while he untied General. David gave her a leg up, and she settled into the saddle. The stirrups were still adjusted for her, since in his haste to find her, David had hopped on General as he was. Now David climbed on behind the saddle and cuddled her in his strong arms. Happily she leaned back into them and let him nuzzle her neck.

''Okay, honey, let's take it slow now,'' he said close to her ear. ''We don't want to both wind up in the mud.''

She smiled with true joy. There were worse things than falling off a horse—even in the mud. She cued General, and they began walking back through the woods, back to the barn and the beginning of a new and trusting stable relationship.